WITHDRAWN

SPECIAL MESSAGE TO READERS

THE ULVERSCROFT FOUNDATION
(registered UK charity number 264873)

was established in 1972 to provide funds for research, diagnosis and treatment of eye diseases. Examples of major projects funded by the Ulverscroft Foundation are:-

- The Children's Eye Unit at Moorfields Eye Hospital, London
- The Ulverscroft Children's Eye Unit at Great Ormond Street Hospital for Sick Children
- Funding research into eye diseases and treatment at the Department of Ophthalmology, University of Leicester
- The Ulverscroft Vision Research Group, Institute of Child Health
- Twin operating theatres at the Western Ophthalmic Hospital, London
- The Chair of Ophthalmology at the Royal Australian College of Ophthalmologists

You can help further the work of the Foundation by making a donation or leaving a legacy. Every contribution is gratefully received. If you would like to help support the Foundation or require further information, please contact:

THE ULVERSCROFT FOUNDATION
The Green, Bradgate Road, Anstey
Leicester LE7 7FU, England
Tel: (0116) 236 4325

website: www.foundation.ulverscroft.com

STANDING THE TEST
OF TIME

When Grace Taylor wins a scholarship to study music at the exclusive Henry Tyndale School, she is determined to work hard to realise her dream of becoming a professional musician. There she meets the charming young Adam, and it feels like they were meant for each other — until a vicious bully with a wealthy father, to whom the school is beholden, succeeds in breaking them apart . . . Eight years later, fate throws Grace and Adam together again. Can they overcome the shadows of the past and make a life together?

SARAH PURDUE

—————◆—————

STANDING THE TEST OF TIME

Complete and Unabridged

LINFORD
Leicester

First published in Great Britain in 2015

First Linford Edition
published 2016

Copyright © 2015 by Sarah Purdue
All rights reserved

A catalogue record for this book is available
from the British Library.

ISBN 978-1-4448-3090-3

Published by
F. A. Thorpe (Publishing)
Anstey, Leicestershire

Set by Words & Graphics Ltd.
Anstey, Leicestershire
Printed and bound in Great Britain by
T. J. International Ltd., Padstow, Cornwall

This book is printed on acid-free paper

The Past

1

He appeared out of nowhere, like Superman. The wheels of the taxi squealed as it came to a shuddering sideways stop. Although she was not hurt, Grace felt as if she couldn't breathe. The view out of the taxi windscreen seemed frozen, like a Christmas tableau. He stood just centimetres from the front of the taxi, with his arms wrapped tightly around the chest of a young boy. Grace felt as if she were under his spell and she could not look away. His gaze was firmly fixed on her and she wondered if he could feel it too — the pull on every part of her; it was like she knew him and had known him for all of her life.

'You all right, miss?' The taxi driver's voice pierced into her consciousness as she realised he had asked her several times.

'I'm fine,' she answered, still unable to take her gaze away from the scene.

It was as if a director had cried 'action'. The taxi driver pushed opened his door and stepped out. The boy was spun round by his saviour and checked for injuries, then drawn into a quick, tight hug. Now others joined the scene. An older man, perhaps the boy's father, pulled him onto the pavement and repeated the exercise of checking for injuries, but it was clear that this man knew what he was looking for. Grace watched, and it was like her brain could finally process what she had seen. Her Superman was in fact an older teenage boy, about her age. He was casually dressed in jeans and a checked shirt over a white T-shirt, but somehow he oozed an expensive sophistication which, even to Grace's inexperienced eye, said that he was from money. She stepped out of the taxi, feeling a little ashamed that she had not offered to help earlier.

'You were supposed to keep an eye on him, Adam. I ask you to do one simple task and you apparently are unable to manage even that. He could have been seriously injured, for god's sake!'

Grace turned her eyes away; she had never enjoyed the sensation of watching another person be embarrassed. She thought she had seen a fleeting look of gratefulness from Adam but wondered if she had imagined it.

'I'm sorry, Father,' Adam began.

'It's not *Adam's* fault, Daddy. I didn't want to be late. Now I'm a junior, I'm supposed to show the new kids to their rooms. It's an important job, you know.'

The older man smiled. 'Well, no harm done, I suppose. But you really must be more careful, Seb. Just because I'm a doctor doesn't mean that I want to spend any more time than absolutely necessary in sorting you out.'

Sebastian tipped his grey school cap and made a big show of looking both ways before darting across the wide gravelled drive.

'Are you injured?' came Adam's voice.

5

Grace was startled from her reverie and felt colour rise a little in her cheeks as she realised that her usual habit of people-watching had been noticed. Her eyes met his, and once again she felt a pull in the pit of her stomach. His eyes were crystal-blue and seemed to have a depth that was not reflected by his age. She shook herself and answered.

'I'm absolutely fine, thank you.' She managed a smile and tilted her head to allow her fringe to fall and hopefully shield some of her redness.

'You must be a new girl; I haven't seen you here before.' Adam held out his hand, and Grace, not knowing what else to do, took it. It was warm and slightly rough. She couldn't remember the last person she had shaken hands with; it wasn't exactly common practice at her last school.

'Joining the sixth form,' she said, forcing herself to look at him. She was struck again by his features. Her original assessment that he was Superman was not far off. He had broad shoulders and a sporty build that suggested he played football, or more likely rugby, since he was at a private school. His eyes seemed to study her face, and there was an openness that surprised her. Was he interested in what she had to say, or merely well-mannered?

'I have a music scholarship, to study . . . well, music,' she added awkwardly, mentally rolling her eyes before returning to stare at the ground.

'Interesting,' he said, with a smile guaranteed to melt the hardest of hearts. Grace suspected it was well-employed to get the bearer out of all manner of trouble.

'The young lady has said she is quite well, Adam. We really must be getting along. I have a full list this afternoon.'

'Of course, Father,' he answered, but his eyes were still firmly fixed on Grace's face. 'I am sure our paths will cross again. I'm in the lower sixth, too.' He dipped his head slightly in a gallant nod and then departed with his father. Grace watched as they crossed the driveway and walked towards the gothic ivy-strung archway that led to The Henry Tyndale Independent School.

'Do you want to get back in, love?' the taxi driver asked. 'I can't see you dragging that trunk of yours all the way up to the main building.'

Grace nodded and got back into the passenger seat.

The taxi drew up in front of an exquisite mansion house. It sat proudly on the wide circular drive as if it were certain of its own importance. There were rows of sash windows gazing out over an immaculately manicured lawn and closely tended rose beds. There were several groups of children, all in varying sorts of school uniform. Some wore caps or straw hats with grey shorts or pinafores. A group of teenagers wore long trousers or short skirts, with identical blazers bearing the school badge and green edging.

As the taxi pulled to a stop behind a row of Range Rovers and BMWs, Grace remembered the last time she had been here. The Louisa Campbell-Green Scholarship for young musicians was highly prized and oversubscribed. Grace had had to endure rounds of musical auditions, on all three of her instruments, not to mention a gruelling entrance exam and an interview with a panel of teachers and governors from the school. It had all been worth it, of course, for this moment. Henry Tyndale offered the best music teachers in the country. This was the moment that signalled the start of the journey to her dream: a place at the Royal Academy of Music. She felt the need to pinch herself. She had done it; she was finally here! For the past ten years, every single winner of the Campbell-Green scholarship had won a coveted place at the Academy, and the oldest five now had distinguished careers in classical music.

The taxi driver was struggling to prise the heavy trunk from the boot and Grace went round to help him. Between them, they managed to manhandle it to the edge of the boot before half-lifting, half-dropping it to the floor. The driver smiled in thanks, but Grace's attention was drawn by the sound of laughter. It was high and light, yet somehow pointed. She scanned the busy driveway and spotted a group of older girls. They wore their skirts as short as regulations would allow, give or take an inch. They had immaculate hair, nails and makeup. They oozed sophistication, style and, not surprisingly, money.

The ringleader of the group gave her a cool stare. 'No need to guess who the latest charity girl is,' she said, looking straight at Grace but directing the comment to her group of girls, whose only aim in life appeared to be to look identical to their leader. She smiled at Grace, but there was no warmth in her eyes. 'Helping the help? Really.' She shook her head in mock disappointment. 'You'd think she'd try harder to at least look like Tyndale material.'

Grace could feel the colour rise in her cheeks. She wanted to answer back but knew it was pointless. She had met bullies before, and since getting a rise out of their victims was what they were after, Grace chose to ignore them.

'Deaf as well. Dear me, they really do give out scholarships to any old waif and stray.' This stinging remark was accompanied by obligatory giggles from the group. Grace turned to take the two cases that contained her flute and violin from the taxi driver.

'Good luck, love, and keep your head held high.' With a wink and a smile, he was gone.

Tightening the grip on her violin case, she looked around for some idea of what she was supposed to do now. She spotted an older woman in what looked like an old-fashioned nurse's uniform holding a clipboard in one hand as she gave some directions to a couple with a small boy in tow. Grace walked over and waited patiently for her to finish.

'Yes, dear. I imagine you are Grace Taylor?'

Grace frowned. Did everyone know who she was?

The older woman smiled. 'A process of elimination. Don't look so worried! You are the only senior joining us this year who hasn't attended the lower school. I'm Harriet Fields, the school matron. Welcome to the Henry Tyndale School. One of the juniors will show you to your room. You'll find that the rest of your luggage has already been delivered. Supper is at six o'clock in the dining room; your roommate will show you where that is.' She smiled kindly before turning to the next child in a queue of juniors waiting to be guides. 'Sebastian, could you show Grace to room four in the west wing, please?'

Grace couldn't help smiling at the young boy who had nearly met his end in front of her taxi.

'Hello again,' he said with a grin. 'If you'll follow me?'

He doffed his cap at her, and despite herself, Grace found herself laughing, the image of the taunting girls fading slightly. She felt a small glow of hope. Perhaps there would be some people here she could be friends with. Her mind drifted back to Sebastian's dramatic rescue, and more importantly his rescuer — the handsome Adam.

'Grace?' She was shaken from her memories by Seb, who stood with his back to a heavy wooden door. It clearly was taking some effort to hold the door open, and Grace was so caught up in her thoughts of Adam that she was simply standing there and letting him. She shook her head.

'Sorry, Sebastian. Lots to take in.'

Seb gave her a cheeky grin, as if he could read her thoughts. 'You'll soon get used it. I wasn't sure at first, but now I can't imagine going to school anywhere else. Course, I had Adam looking out for me. He's my big brother,' he added unnecessarily.

'How old were you when you started here?' Grace asked as they made their way up a wide marble staircase that showed the wear of thousands of shoes and boots.

'Seven,' he said matter-of-factly.

Grace was a bit shocked. She couldn't imagine leaving home to live at school at such a young age.

'I would have come earlier, but I couldn't,' Seb added. Grace looked at him questioningly. 'Too poorly,' he explained with a shrug.

Grace nodded as if she understood. Perhaps he did not want to admit to being too afraid to come away to school before then.

Seb pushed through a set of double doors and indicated the third in a row of wooden doors. This one had a nameplate on it with a hand-written label: 'Rebecca Goldberg and Grace Taylor'.

'Becky will tell you where to go for supper and anything else you need to know,' said Seb. 'You could ask me, too, since I've been here longer than you,' he added with a tinge of pride.

'I will,' Grace reassured him. 'Thanks for your help.'

He grinned back. 'No problem. And you can always ask Adam. He likes you,

I can tell.' Seb's grin broadened, and then he disappeared back through the double doors.

2

Grace unpacked. There was no sign of her roommate, so when a bell rang she followed the crowds in the direction of dinner. The dining hall was as grand as she imagined one in an ancestral home would be: the walls were lined with dark wood and the large windows filled with stained glass bearing the family's coat of arms and depicting various images of Tyndales undertaking heroic deeds. It was all so stereotypical of a 'posh school' that Grace had to hold back a giggle, deciding it would be one of the first things to be included in her letter home.

The hall was lined with several long tables, which were occupied by younger children in uniform. It didn't take Grace long to work out that she didn't belong there. Towards the front of the hall was a table occupied by teachers

16

decked out in black gowns, while the older students were sitting at smaller tables in groups. Grace tried to ignore the stares and whispered snatches of conversation. She walked slowly towards the tables, hoping to spot a space where she could quickly sit down and avoid further attention.

A girl with long black hair raised a perfectly manicured hand. 'There's a space here, if you like?' Her voice was cultured, with a hint of a French accent.

Grace smiled gratefully and moved towards the space. She had just reached the table when its occupants spread out on the bench, ensuring there was nowhere she could sit.

'My apologies,' said the black-haired girl. 'I thought you were someone else. We don't do charity here.'

Despite her best efforts, Grace could feel colour rising in her cheeks, worsened by the sound of spiteful laughter. She moved quickly to the table furthest away from the group and sat down. The laughter continued ringing in her ears, and she was aware that the occupants of her table were now appraising her reaction. Thinking back to the taxi driver's advice to hold her head up, she lifted her gaze from her study of the cutlery and looked in the direction of the laughter. The black-haired girl and her companions were staring at her, and she met their gaze evenly, trying to convey that their words had no effect. The black-haired girl looked away first, turning her head to her neighbour. Grace's heart stopped as she recognised Adam. The black-haired girl slipped her arm through both of his, which were folded on the table. He bent his head so he could hear what she said, but Grace could feel him looking at her. The girl said something which Grace could not make out, and he joined in with the raucous laughter that ensued.

Grace couldn't help but look away now, somehow disappointed in him and resigning herself to the fact that she could not trust first impressions. He was one of 'them' — a popular kid; and by the looks of it, he was *the* popular kid: the one who everyone else longed to be, and would do anything to be noticed by.

Grace was grateful when the hall fell silent; then there was the sound of scraping of chairs as the students stood up as one. Her eyes drifted back to the table of her tormentors and, for the briefest second, locked with Adam's. She thought she saw a flicker of regret or sympathy. But it was over almost before it began, and it was to keep her mind occupied through the meal as she tried to work out if she had imagined it or not. There was something about this boy that drew her in — a fact that she found more than faintly ridiculous since she had met him only once and had had the briefest of conversations. Also, he was clearly part of an 'in' crowd that she had no desire, let alone chance, to be part of. Still, there was something . . . she was sure of it.

After dinner, she went in search of the practice room where all music instruments were to be stored. She had decided against asking anyone and instead was relying on her memory of her tour of the school. She had not been impressed by the grand entrance or the teachers in their black gowns. What *had* impressed her were the music practice rooms. There were eight, all containing a baby grand piano, various music stands and a library of sheet music. The music rooms formed a corridor, but no noise could be heard from here as the rooms were well sound-proofed.

After several wrong turns, Grace found the corridor that she knew would be her home away from home. There was no sound: it was the silence that gave it away. She reached out a hand for the handle of the first door and found that the 'vacant' sign had been covered with an 'engaged' sign. When she reached the final practice room, she was dismayed to find that it, like all the others, was already taken. She knew that the school prided itself in the musical abilities of its students; clearly the students themselves took that reputation seriously too.

Grace allowed her cello case to slip from her shoulder, and sighed. This was not going to be easy. She was desperate for the comfort of playing something from home. She stared down the corridor and saw one final door, which had definitely not been on the grand tour. Walking towards it, she smiled as the she saw that the 'vacant' sign remained uncovered. She pushed it open with one hand.

Once inside, she could tell instantly that the room was rarely used and quite possibly forgotten by everyone else. She smiled; she had found her own personal hideaway, where she could practise without being disturbed and forget about the world that lay outside the door. The room smelt musty and unimportant, much like how she felt herself. She shook head, throwing off the self-pity. This was what she had wanted — and no one, particularly not a group of stuck-up, spoilt teenagers, was going to ruin it for her!

The curtains at the small window were a crushed deep-blue velvet and reminded Grace of cinemas from years gone by. At one end there was what seemed to be an old stage, piled high with old props and costumes, long since forgotten. The piano was an old upright that clearly still got tuned regularly. The keys were slightly worn and were somehow softer to the touch.

She knew she should practise the complicated piece her piano teacher had assigned her in her last lesson, but she felt suddenly homesick and instead played her mum's favourite piece. Lost in the music, she closed her eyes, the piece so familiar that she did not need the score, or to watch her fingers. She was transported to her elderly piano at home that was squeezed into one corner of the kitchen/dining room of her parents' terraced house. She could almost smell her mum cooking her favourite dinner, spaghetti carbonara, and chatting to her dad about their days at work. When she finished, she paused for the inevitable applause that her parents always showered upon her, no matter what she played or however well she did it.

She was just about to launch into another favourite piece when a stilted clapping made her freeze. She swivelled on her piano stool and scanned the room for the previously unseen occupant.

'You play very well,' a lazy voice said from the stage. Adam was lounging across a pile of old costumes. He had shed his school uniform for jeans and oversized shirt.

Grace could feel colour rise in her face, and then anger. She wondered if the other members of his little clique were hiding behind the curtains, just waiting for the opportunity to continue tormenting her. But there was also fear: fear that her new hiding place had been discovered — this room, that she had so quickly begun to see as *her* room, and that she had hoped would be her sanctuary.

'What are you doing here?' She inwardly winced at her accusatory tone; this was not the way to deal with a 'cool' kid.

'Why, do you own this place? I didn't see your name on the door.' His expression was neutral, but Grace still felt a prickle of anger.

'No name, but perhaps you missed the 'occupied' sign?' She raised one eyebrow in what she hoped was an expression of cool disinterest. She had been taken with this boy's charm at their first meeting, but he had shown his true colours just hours later. She could feel his eyes on her, and forced herself to look back at him, with all emotion hidden from her face. He appeared to be studying her — whether looking for weakness, or out of interest, Grace couldn't be sure.

★　★　★

'Has it occurred to you that I may have been here first?' He stood up from his lounging place and took a slow, measured step towards her.

Grace flushed again and put a hand instinctively to her neck to try and hide it. 'No. But if you were here, you should have changed the sign on the door.' She frowned, wondering how she had missed his presence. 'Anyway, this is a practice room, and I don't see you playing any instruments.'

'I'll have you know I am a serious musician.' His face was definitely mocking now.

'Really,' she said. It was more of a statement than a question.

'Yes. Would you like to hear me play?'

'Be my guest,' Grace answered with a wave of a hand, as if she were a conductor.

Adam made a great show of standing up straight, smoothing down the front of his shirt and coughing to clear his throat. Out of his pocket he pulled something thin and green. Grace fought

25

back a smile as she realised it was a blade of grass. Adam looked her directly in the eye and she held his gaze for a moment, trying to ignore her heart fluttering in her chest. He launched into a concerto playing of the school song, managing to complete all nine verses before collapsing back on the pile of costumes with a very red face, puffing as if he had run a marathon.

Grace could not help herself — she giggled and clapped her hands before calling, 'Encore, encore!'

Adam pulled himself up and dropped into an exaggerated bow. What was she doing, and what was she thinking? She forced herself to relive the mortifying moment when she had tried to sit down with his cronies, and their loud and public rejection. She remembered his face and his silence. He hadn't leapt to her defence; had not even acknowledged that they had met! She wasn't some foolish teenager who swooned at the first boy who gave her any attention, good or bad. She was here to study music; to follow her dream! She forced the smile from her face, trying for coolly detached once more.

'Alas, I fear that I am spent, but we have other musical talent in the room — perhaps she would like to entertain us?' Adam either hadn't noticed that he had lost his audience, or he didn't care. He held out his hand, and Grace waited a moment, inwardly trying to work out just what was going on. With a sigh, she allowed him to take her hand and lead her back to the piano stool.

She sat and then wriggled along the stool as it became clear that he was going to sit next to her. She placed her fingers over the keys and then paused. Perhaps she should call him out; make it clear that she was no fool and was not about to willingly give him ammunition for her future misery.

'Silence can be musical, I suppose, but I was rather hoping you would play it rather than stare at it.' His face showed amusement. What if he genuinely wanted to hear her play? What if he had felt it, too — that tug, that flutter of something, that she couldn't describe when she saw him?

'Why are you here?' she asked in little more than a whisper.

'Well, I was hoping to hear you play,' he whispered back, and she could feel his warm breath on her ear.

She forced herself to look him in the eye, and saw questioning rather than mocking. 'Is this some kind of trick?' She was embarrassed at the pleading in her voice. There was a part of her that desperately wished it was real; that her feelings, new and unfamiliar, had not misled her.

He seemed genuinely puzzled, but that was not to be relied upon. 'What kind of trick would I need to get you to play?'

Grace had no idea how to explain her fears. If she were wrong, she would look a complete idiot; but she couldn't help glancing around the room and wondering if others were hidden there. Adam seemed to track her gaze.

'We are alone, you know. You'd only be playing for me.' He still looked slightly puzzled, and for a moment Grace hoped he would think she was merely suffering from stage fright.

Her fingers felt their way to the right keys, and she played. She tried to pretend that Adam was not there — that it was just her and the empty practice room; but she could not shake off his warm presence next to her. He sat completely still, as if he were afraid to disturb her. More than that, he seemed to really listen, his head tilted slightly to one side. It was a sad piece that spoke of sorrow and loss. Grace's hands played the last notes, and then there was silence.

They sat next to each other for what felt like an age. The stillness between them was a comfortable silence, and neither wanted to break the spell. The discomfort that Grace had felt at Adam's closeness was gone. Instead, she longed for him to move nearer; for their arms to touch. She knew that whatever his intentions, she was being incredibly foolish. She had not yet been here a whole day, and already she had allowed herself to be distracted from the only reason she was here. If he were playing her, she would live to regret it in the days to come. And if he wasn't? Well, that was even more frightening.

It had never bothered her before; she had always told herself that there was plenty of time for romance when she had achieved what she wanted. But she had never felt like this before. She had been so dismissive of her friends, who seemed to fall so easily for boys who showed them a passing interest — but now she knew how they felt. Adam's presence seemed to drive all common sense from Grace's head, and what she wanted was to be near him. She wondered if he felt the same, and was surprised and maybe unnerved by it too. She did not want to break the magical silence, but she knew that she could not wait for him to speak; she had to ask if he felt that way too. The boldness was new to her; she was someone who carried her heart and feelings so close to her chest that even her family didn't really know what she was thinking.

Adam's wrist bleeped and he looked at his watch. He sighed and then stood up. 'I have to go.'

Grace knew that she had her answer. He was leaving. If he felt something, he was not interested. He might yet be collecting evidence to cause her pain. 'Okay,' she said, although she felt anything but. She fought to keep her emotions in. She was just homesick, she told herself. Tomorrow she would feel different. She would forget this moment and throw herself into her music.

She started as Adam placed his hand gently on her arm, which was resting on the piano keys. She didn't trust herself to look at him, knowing that her face would be as readable as a child's picture book. He sighed and then he was gone. He sighed! The thought excited her, but moments later the feelings of foolishness returned. She was not some poorly educated girl in a regency romance!

She pulled the most challenging piece of music from her bag, set it on the piano stand and started to play, forcing all other thoughts from her mind.

3

Grace could not quite believe she had been at Henry Tyndale for two whole weeks. It felt like a lifetime. Everything at the school was so different from what she was used to. Even the unwritten rules that governed groups of teenagers seemed to be totally foreign. In some ways it was just the same: you had the popular kids, the extremely unpopular kids and then the largest group, which formed the middle ground, most of whom worked hard to be in the former and even harder to avoid being in the latter. In her last school, Grace had been in the middle group and had been quite happy with her lot in life. But at Henry Tyndale she found herself in the extremely unpopular group, and the only apparent reason was her comparatively humble background. She told herself that she would not be ashamed of where she came from and who she was, but this did not take away the minute-by-minute agony of being the daily verbal punching bag of a group of girls she had nicknamed the Barnacles. They dressed, thought and acted the same as each other, or at least the same as the leader of the group — the black-haired girl who had taunted Grace outside the school on her first day and refused her a seat in the dining room.

Arabella was the unmistakable leader of the Barnacles. She was always immaculately made up, and effortlessly clever — particularly at languages, since her father was an ambassador. Before starting school, Arabella had lived all over the world. Her faint accent seemed to give her an exotic appeal, and her jet-setting lifestyle and wide range of experiences made her the flame to the other girls' moths. Grace was on the whole unimpressed by the cruel girl, except perhaps for her ability to be a master manipulator one minute and sweetness and light the next — usually when a teacher was nearby.

Grace picked up her pen again before gazing out of the tall bay window. She was snugly tucked away behind the great deep-red brocade curtains that hung from floor to ceiling. If she pulled her feet in tightly, she could not be seen from the wide, sunny lower-sixth common room. Looking out of the west side, Grace could see the boys' junior rugby and football teams practising whilst the older boys ran warm-up laps around the fields, waiting for their turn to play. A familiar shape was out in front, his hair flopping over one eye and his arms pumping firmly. Grace could feel the now-familiar tingle of excitement when she saw him, and for once she indulged herself, smiling, confident that no one could see her face or the feelings it showed. Her mind wandered into an imaginary world where he might look up and smile and wave at her.

Grace had not seen Adam alone since

that first night in the music room. A small part of her wanted him to join her there again, but with time her hopes had faded, and she was left with the dull ache of disappointment. She told herself it was a good thing, and that she needed to focus on her music. She had given up so much to be here, and she knew that in order to keep her place she needed to continue to impress, both academically and musically. She glanced at her watch; she had spent over an hour writing her letter, and she needed to get back to her homework.

After the informal supper that set apart Saturday evenings from every other, Grace made her way to her music room. On Monday evening the orchestra was going to start work on a new piece. Mr Doucette, her Italian music teacher, had assigned her the second violin seat, and she was determined to show him that she was more than up to the task. The corridor was quiet, and her room had the now-familiar 'vacant' sign on display. She pushed it across so it read 'engaged', and entered the room.

Inside, it was still and quiet. Despite herself, the question still formed in Grace's mind — was Adam there?

'Of course not,' she said abruptly, putting down her case and unclasping the clips.

'You do know that talking to yourself is the first sign of madness?' The voice was warm and not at all mocking. Grace tried not to smile but failed.

'I believe the real issue is if you start answering yourself,' she retorted, and stuck out her tongue ,at Adam, who appeared from his hiding place at the back of the small stage. 'Why are you here?'

He turned his head to one side and studied her face. She raised her eyebrows but made no comment, wanting to see what he had to say for himself. 'I couldn't stay away. I washed up after practice and had an overwhelming desire to hear beautiful music.'

Grace frowned, wondering if he meant what he said.

'That was supposed to be a compliment,' he said mildly, and Grace wondered if he could read her mind.

'I never had you pegged as a lover of classical music,' she said, to hide her confused emotions.

'Maybe not publicly.' Adam let the statement hang in the air, and Grace wondered if he were trying to explain why he never spoke to her in public and why he never defended her from her tormentors.

'It would seem that's not the only thing you don't support in public.' She knew it was a barbed comment, but she couldn't just flit from being friends, or whatever this was, to strangers when it suited him. She had not allowed herself to dwell on it, but his blankness was hurtful and not something that could simply be glossed over by his charm.

The amusement left his face and he became serious. He walked over and sat on the piano stool, his back to the instrument, facing her. 'I'm sorry,' he said.

It was such a simple statement, and it hung in the air. Grace swallowed the lump that had appeared in her throat and willed herself not to cry. 'Are you,' she said. It was a statement rather than a question. Did it matter that he was sorry? she asked herself. Being sorry didn't change the fact that the Barnacles tormented her daily. Surely if he were genuinely sorry, he would do something about it!

She picked up her violin and began to lightly twist the pegs for each string before tuning them. She could feel Adam watching her closely, but concentrated on the task. It was his job to make the first move.

'I hate this school,' he said softly.

Grace looked up. This wasn't exactly what she was expecting.

'It's all so false,' he added, as if this were explanation enough.

Grace threw him a querying look before tuning the final string.

He stood and began to pace. 'Everything about this place is for appearances — the way we dress, the way we're supposed to act. I hate it.' He brought a fist down on the top of the piano, and a low rumbling noise issued from it as if in complaint. Adam and Grace exchanged glances and could not help the laughter that resulted.

'I'm not sure if that piano is in agreement with you or not, but I don't think you should beat it any more,' Grace said between giggles.

'Sorry,' Adam said, addressing the piano. 'I shouldn't be taking it out on you.' He turned to Grace. 'Or you.'

Silence stretched out between them.

'I want to say that it's okay, Adam, but I can't because . . . well, it isn't,' Grace answered honestly.

'I know, I know,' Adam said, running a hand through his hair. For a moment he looked younger than his sixteen years. 'I know it's not okay, and I shouldn't be asking you to say that it is.' He looked at her helplessly.

'Tell me,' she said. 'Tell me why you ignore me. Why you ignore what your friends say and do.' She could feel her cheeks pinking up at the memories that came flooding back.

Adam moved to stand nearer to her, and she had to fight the urge to reach out and touch him. 'They're not my friends — not really. They'd turn on me as soon as look at me if my situation changed.'

'So that's why,' Grace said. She was disappointed somehow, although she had always expected that this was the truth. 'Your reputation is more important. I understand.' She lifted her violin to her chin and picked up her bow. She would not waste any more time on this boy.

Adam reached out a hand and gently took her violin before placing it carefully back in its case. He pulled her free hand and she followed him to the pile of old costumes, which formed a sort of collapsed sofa. They both sat.

'I haven't been able to think of anything else for the past two weeks,' Adam said. 'It's always felt false here, but I just figured that was life and I should accept it. Just two more years and I'd be out of here.' He looked at Grace earnestly now, and she nodded to indicate she was listening. 'Then you came along. So fearless. Letting no one dictate to you who you are or what you want from life. Being prepared to take insults and shrug them off.'

Grace shook her head. That was so far from the truth!

He studied her again. 'Or perhaps not.'

Grace did not try to fight the tears that welled up and ran down her face. Adam lifted a hand and with one thumb brushed her cheek.

'But despite that, you haven't changed, Grace. You don't allow it to define you. You refused to change yourself to fit some sort of warped social hierarchy that demands you conform. You are the most courageous person I've ever met, and you put me to shame.'

Grace looked into Adam's eyes and saw again what she had known at their first meeting. He was different; there was more to him than could be seen on the outside. There was also a connection between them, unspoken, and Grace knew that she would never be able to put it into words.

'I am so, so sorry, Grace,' Adam said. Then he pulled her into his arms. Grace let her head rest against his chest, and for the first time since she had arrived, she allowed herself to cry. All the bitterness and hurt just poured from her as Adam rocked her gently and murmured into her hair.

4

They sat together like that for what felt
like an age. Grace closed her eyes and
enjoyed the sensation of being held as if
she were precious and important. She
wondered if life would be different now.
Anyone could say sorry, and even genuinely mean it, but it did not necessarily
follow that that person had the strength
to change.

'How are you feeling?' Adam asked
quietly.

'Hungry,' she said, and then laughed;
it had been the first thing that sprang to
mind.

'In that case, it's a good job I have a
secret stash of supplies.' He gently
pulled his arm away and got to his feet.
There was some rustling behind the
stage, and then he reappeared with a
triumphant grin. 'What would made-
moiselle prefer? We have here an

44

exceptional traditional lemonade, or if you have more expensive tastes we do a fine line in lager shandy.'

Grace giggled. 'Lemonade, please.'

Adam tugged on the ring-pull and then handed her the drink. She took a grateful sip and watched as he pulled the ring from his own can of lager shandy, then raised an eyebrow.

'It's only one percent alcohol,' he said. 'There's no need to be so disapproving.'

Grace smiled. 'Sorry. Just don't want you to get into trouble. It *is* against school rules,' she added in mock-seriousness.

Adam snorted. 'Stuff school rules!' He raised his can in mock salutation. 'Here's to the one place where school rules need not apply.'

Grace lifted her can and clunked it against his, and they both laughed. She thought for a moment. 'Here's to the one place where we can both be ourselves.' She raised her can again, and Adam joined her in the toast.

'Amen to that,' he said, which made Grace laugh once more. 'I also have . . .' He paused as if waiting for a drum roll. ' . . . dolly mixture!'

Grace grabbed the packet out of his hand — her absolute favourite! 'How did you know?' she asked with an air of suspicion.

'I can never reveal my sources, not even on pain of death.' He raised an eyebrow.

Grace sat up. 'Really?' she said, eyeing him like a cat with a baby bird.

Adam opened his mouth to speak, but no words came as he found himself laughing helplessly due to a sudden onslaught of tickles. Grace had a sense that he was ticklish and so went for his side and behind his knees. Adam kicked out and tried to get away, but was somewhat hindered by his helpless laughter. With some effort, he reached out and started to tickle back. They rolled over, clutching their aching sides.

'Stop!' Adam gasped between trying to breathe and trying to laugh. 'I surrender. I'll tell you all — just stop this torture.'

Grace withdrew and tried to catch her breath as well, but was prepared when Adam launched a cowardly attack. 'You said stop! You're such a cheat.' She rolled onto one side and out of reach, then held up one hand whilst the other gripped her side as she tried to still the pain from her laughter-exhausted muscles.

Adam joined her, lying beside her so that their shoulders and elbows touched. He reached out and felt for her hand, then held it gently. 'Before you arrived I put a small video camera in the door-knob of your wardrobe,' he said with a grin.

Grace pulled away with such a look of horror on her face that it brought Adam up short.

'I'm joking,' he said, holding out both palms to placate her. 'Really, just joking, I promise.' When he saw that her face was still clouded with suspicion and concern, he smiled sadly. 'I would never do that,' he insisted. 'It was Seb — I asked him to see if he could find out what you liked. Of course, I was thinking more along the lines of bands, TV programmes and stuff; but he told me that he'd seen you open a parcel in the porter's office and that it contained dolly mixture.' He carefully watched for signs that she might believe him, and was rewarded with the glimmer of a smile. 'Seb said he'd never seen anyone get so excited over kiddies' sweets, and that you must be addicted or something.'

Now Grace really did smile. She could remember that day, her third day at Henry Tyndale. She had received a note to say that a parcel had arrived for her that was too big to fit in her pigeonhole where all her mail normally went. She also remembered the cheeky grin of Seb, who had caught her dancing around with the box in her arms.

'Thank you,' she said, and she really meant it. Clearly Adam cared — perhaps only a little, but enough to try and find out more about her. She pulled open the packet and made a face as he made a careful search and pulled out a yellow jelly. She watched as he carefully and deliberately put it in his mouth, savouring it as if he were tasting the costliest caviar. Without warning, he reached over and snatched the packet from her hands and started to pick out the yellow jellies. Grace reached up to reclaim her prize, but Adam jumped to his feet and held the packet high over his head, well out of her reach. She made a jump for it, arms outstretched, and somehow they found themselves collapsed in a heap, arms and legs intertwined.

'You are the most real girl in this school,' Adam whispered, his face so close to hers that she could feel his breath on her cheek. He reached up a hand and brushed a lock of her hair from her face. 'I'm sorry for everything, and I promise you it'll be different from now on.'

Grace smiled sadly. 'Easy to say,

Adam,' she whispered back. Her eyes were locked on his, and she felt like she was losing part of herself into their depths.

He moved closer and brushed his lips against hers, gently, as if he didn't want to frighten her. Feelings rushed through her, all jumbled up and confusing. A fleeting thought that she was being taken for a ride, that this was a trick, buzzed in her mind. Firmly she pushed it away. Whatever happened in the future didn't matter. She knew what she wanted right now. Right now she wanted to kiss him; to be kissed by him. She wanted to share her first proper kiss with Adam.

He moved away slightly as if checking for her permission. This time it was Grace who moved. Gently, she returned the kiss, her eyes still locked with his. The kiss deepened and Grace closed her eyes, giving herself completely to the moment.

5

Grace felt like she was frozen in the most perfect moment of her life. She felt as if an orchestra were playing and her soul was soaring above it. Adam's hands held her face to his, and her skin felt alive as if he were kissing every part of her at once. A beep sounded in her ear, which she ignored; but she felt Adam's body tense slightly, and with a sigh he drew away.

'I have to go. Sorry.' His voice was slightly hoarse and filled with regret. He went to move away, but Grace reached out for his arm and pulled his wrist towards her.

'What is it?' she asked.

'A watch, Gracie. I assume you have seen one before.'

She frowned in mock irritation, but inside she felt alive at the sound of her name changed affectionately by him.

She raised an eyebrow.

Adam sat up slowly, his eyes fixed on her face, and she could see sorrow and worry roll across him. 'It's Seb. He's sick.'

Grace sat up now, too, and reached for his hand.

'Seb has cystic fibrosis.'

Her eyes widened in shock. When Seb had told her on her first day that he'd been too poorly to start school, she had assumed he was covering up for not wanting to come earlier, or at worst some minor ailment.

'I can tell by your expression that you know what it is and what it means.'

Grace nodded. 'But he looks so well,' she said, feeling foolish.

Adam smiled. 'He is right now, thank god. But don't let Seb fool you; he's a master at hiding it for as long as he can. I'm pretty good at telling when he's in for a bad time. But . . . ' He shrugged, and there was an element of despair in him that made Grace want to pull him tightly to her.

'And the watch?' she asked.

'Seb needs physio to keep his chest clear; it's his best chance to keep well. My father employs someone to come in three times a day, but Seb prefers me to do it if I can, so I always do the evening one. Also, it means I can set up his feed.'

Grace took a moment to take all this in.

'So I have to go. Do you understand?' Adam said, gently removing his hand from hers and standing.

'Of course,' Grace said. Of course she understood. She could see concern in his eyes, as if she would think less of him for this. 'Of course I understand, Adam. He's your brother, and a great kid,' she added with a smile.

He watched her closely, and she stood on her tiptoes to kiss him. She broke away first, knowing that he needed to go. 'Go on,' she said, 'and say hi to Seb for me.'

He moved towards the door and then stopped. Slowly, he turned around. 'It'll be different tomorrow, I promise. I mean, *I'll* be different.'

He seemed so childlike and unsure in that moment that Grace had to smile. She nodded, not trusting herself to speak, unsure what she would say. Adam hadn't moved, and Grace knew in that moment that he needed her to accept the truth of what he'd said.

'I believe you, Adam.' Saying the words out loud made her feel desperate. She wanted them to be true so badly, but she was afraid of getting hurt. For all that Adam was in this room, out there in the school he was a teenaged boy, trying to survive the experience, just like she was. He remained still, as if he were frozen in time, and Grace wondered if he could read her thoughts; her doubts. She stood up and walked slowly towards him. Carefully standing on tiptoe, she brushed her lips against his, and felt a flash of electricity run through her.

'It's okay,' she said, although whether she was saying it was okay if he couldn't be different or that she truly believed him, she didn't know. 'You have to go.' She smiled up into his face and watched as some of the tension disappeared from around his eyes. He gave her a small grin back before reaching for her face and pulling her into a deep kiss. Grace felt as if every bone in her body had gone soft and that she would simply melt away. When they broke apart, they were both breathless, and Grace could see her own feelings mirrored in Adam's face.

'Seb,' she managed to squeak, and Adam slowly nodded, laughing a little. He dragged his eyes away from her face with a look of deep regret, and then he was gone.

Grace was startled from her reverie by the sound of the school bell. It was now half an hour until all students had to return to their rooms. For the first time in memory, she had not played a single instrument for an entire day. This had never happened before; even on days when she'd been sick, she'd managed at least an hour of practice. Her sensible side was back, berating her and pointing out her own foolishness. She was behaving like some kid who didn't know what she wanted from life. She was different; she had known what she wanted to do since she was five and had her first opportunity to play music. She wanted to go to the Royal College of Music, to learn under the best, and then to play as a professional around the world. She had worked so hard up to this point, made the sacrifices required and turned down opportunities for fun — and the first boy who showed her any attention had caused her, in a day, to discard her dreams.

But then there was the memory of how it felt to be held in someone's arms. How it felt to be loved and to love — and music seemed less important. No, that wasn't true. How she felt actually made the music she played seem more alive, more real. Adam loved her music, too, and loved to hear her play. She was sure he would be equally horrified that she had missed a day's practice. No, she had to find a way — there *had* to be a way to have both music and love in her life. She and Adam could spend some time together, and then when he had to go and take care of Seb she would practise. Perhaps she should even think about getting up earlier to practise in the mornings, too. Surely that would make up for any missed time?

6

Grace's alarm clock sounded and she reached across and silenced it on the first buzz. She had been awake for hours, and no amount of willing would bring back sleep. She stared up at the ceiling, wondering what the day would bring, and feeling an equal mix of excitement and dread. Would today be the first day of her new life here at Tyndale with Adam by her side? Or would the fear of disappointment and hurt win out when Adam continued to behave as if she did not exist outside of their music room? With a sigh, she threw back her covers. There was only one way to find out, and her day would not improve if she received punishment for being late for breakfast.

Hurrying into the dining hall, with her hands trying to tame her hair into a ponytail, Grace bumped into a figure that had seemed to step out of nowhere.

'Careful!' a voice warned.

'Sorry! I wasn't paying . . . ' Grace stopped talking as her brain processed the voice and made the connection.

Adam stood in front of her, one hand on her elbow to prevent her from crashing into the serving counter.

'Clumsy much?' he said, and was rewarded with laughter from the nearby table of Barnacles.

Grace felt her insides freeze up, and the dull pain of false hope started to grow into what she knew was going to be the sharper pain of rejection. She felt Adam's hand move down from her elbow. His touch was in itself painful, and she took a small step back; but before she could escape completely to try and compose herself, she felt his hand on the pocket of her school blazer. She forced herself to look up now, knowing that the Barnacles would be watching their every move.

'May be you should watch where

you're going, too,' she said, making her tone cold and lifeless. Without looking, she knew that her audience had open mouths and wide eyes. Nobody spoke to Adam in this way, not even Arabella.

Grace watched as Adam raised an eyebrow, his face showing signs of anger. He leaned in and Grace could feel his breath on her cheek. 'Pretend I've threatened you,' he whispered. 'Oh, and read the note I've just dropped in your pocket.'

Then he stepped back with the self-satisfied look of a teenager who had scored a point against his enemy. Grace couldn't process what had just happened; couldn't make sense of it or work out whether it was a good or bad thing. Fortunately, the confused look of shock must have been what Adam was after, as he smiled coldly and stepped away from her. She watched as he returned to his seat at the head of the table, everyone there begging to know what he had said. Grace could not hear the words; but when there was a collective howl of laughter, she knew that what he had told them was not remotely similar to what he had whispered to her a moment ago.

She turned her attention to collecting some food for her breakfast. She was desperate to read the note, hopeful that it might give some clue to Adam's behaviour, but equally scared it was just part of a sick game he might be playing to amuse the Barnacles. Her blazer felt heavy on one side, like her pocket was being dragged downwards. She forced herself to take a sip of tea and then turned her attention to her breakfast, forcing herself to eat, knowing when she had she could escape.

Her room felt like a sanctuary in way it had never done before. She sat on the edge of her bed and slowly put her hand in her pocket. The desire to read the note seemed to have left her. What if Adam was just like everyone else, and this note was going to be the final unequivocal evidence of that?

Then she shook herself and mentally

gave herself a quick talking-to. This was just like removing a plaster — best to do it quickly, and get the pain over and done with. The piece of paper had been folded like a work of art into an intricate triangle shape, all tucked in on itself. Not wanting to tear it, she gently eased it apart before opening it out. The first word made her heart bounce in her chest. It had to be a good sign.

'Gracie — I want you to know that I've been thinking all night about the things we said.' Her heart stopped bouncing and seemed to still. She still couldn't tell if this was good news or bad. 'That means you might need to throw something at me in history class to keep me awake!' She smiled now, some relief flowing through her. 'I've been thinking about this place and how it works. I know that Arabella and her cronies make life miserable for you, and I want to make them stop. The thing is, Gracie, I know them, and I think if we are up front about being together it could make it worse for you.'

Grace looked up from the paper and tried to marshal her thoughts. With a deep sigh, she turned back to the note. 'I know what you are thinking — that I'm going back on my word. I'm not, I promise. I just think we need to go about this carefully. I think I can make life better for you from inside her inner circle, so that's what I'm going to do. Please trust me, and meet me in our music room tonight. A.'

Not for the first time, Grace wished that she could talk to her friends. Kate and Paula were self-professed experts on all things boy-related and would at least be able to give advice based on some experience. The problem really came down to trust. Did she trust Adam? She had lain awake pondering that question. She had also wondered what life would be like when the Barnacles found out that she and Adam were together, and doubted very much that she would be welcomed by them with open arms. In fact, she suspected that Adam was right — Arabella and

63

her crowd of wannabes would make her life even more miserable. Despite this, however, Grace allowed herself a little pang of disappointment. Arabella could do her worst, but if Adam was by her side surely that would make everything okay. She knew that was probably unfair on Adam, he had much more to lose than she did. But perhaps he thought she wasn't worth the risk.

The morning had been relatively uneventful; most of her classmates ignored her unless Arabella was feeling in the need for some entertainment. This suited Grace, who kept her head down and focused on her work, pushing Adam far from her mind. The afternoon consisted of ethics and then religious knowledge, and Adam would be in both of her classes. The rest of her timetable was delivered in a formal, traditional manner. However, ethics involved group discussion and much less supervision by the teacher, which gave Arabella ample opportunity to torture her.

Grace took her seat, which she had

carefully chosen as off to one side and near the front. The centre of the front row was reserved for the overly enthusiastic students who seemed one hundred percent focused on their studies, while behind sat the middle group of averagely popular students. The desks at the back were reserved for the most popular ones. Grace's seat off to one side sometimes helped, being out of the line of sight; but if the lesson involved group discussions, she knew she would have to move from the relative safety of her seat to join a group, and most likely she would find herself in Arabella's.

Grace kept her head down as the front row filled. These students would never be late under any circumstances. Other students drifted in, and then finally, like a pack of wolves following the alpha female, the Barnacles arrived. With much attention given to their own importance and superiority to the other students, they took their seats at the back of the class. Grace heard her own name mentioned a few times but blocked out the conversations, as listening to them did little but make her feel small and unimportant despite the fact that she told herself she did not care what they thought.

'Right, I need you in groups of six students, said the teacher, Mr Lombard. 'Arabella, you can be head of one group. Adam, you can be the head of the other.' He looked at the students over his half-moon glasses. 'Well, you know what to do. Get on with it.' His tone moved to exasperation with lightning speed.

There was the sound of scraping chairs as those at the front moved to watch Adam and Arabella, sitting in the back row, make their picks. Grace watched as Arabella fluttered her eyelids at Adam. He rolled his eyes and waved a hand in a gallant way, indicating that she could go first. She took her time and viewed the group of students in front of her. Grace wasn't sure why she bothered with the show, since everyone knew that she would pick the Barnacles in the room before anyone else.

'Grace,' she said. Grace wasn't really listening, as she was never picked until the last student was in a team.

'Grace — wakey, wakey,' Mr Lombard said.

She stood up at the sound of her name, unsure of what to do. She wanted to look to Adam for some indication of what was going on but thought better of it. Carefully she collected her folder and pens and made her way to Arabella's side of the classroom. Arabella patted the seat next to her and smiled, a smile that if Grace didn't know better she would have thought was genuine. She sat down stiffly, unable to read the stares she was getting, particularly from the Barnacles. Either they were great actors, or they were as surprised as she was.

The group was handed its task and, true to form, Arabella started tormenting another girl. Grace found herself having to look away. It was like watching a cat play with a mouse before the inevitable end. From her seat Grace could see Adam, and when she looked away she could feel his gaze. She wondered if Adam had anything to do with Arabella's apparent change of attitude.

'Gracie — may I call you Gracie? It seems so much friendlier than Grace,' Arabella said.

'If you like,' Grace replied noncommittedly, knowing that it would make no difference whether she agreed or not.

'I found this on the message board in the common room. I took it down as soon as I saw it, but I thought I should show it to you.'

Grace watched as Arabella leaned down and pull an A4 sheet of paper from her bag, which she handed over. It was a caricature of her as a homeless person dressed in rags and begging for money.

'I'm so sorry, Grace. It's such a

hateful thing for someone to do.'

Grace could feel Arabella's eyes studying her, and she managed to keep her face neutral. 'It's just a stupid joke,' she said, screwing up the piece of paper.

'Well it's not very funny, if you ask me. You should report it.'

Grace had to work hard to hold in the bitter laugh bubbling up inside her. She was not foolish enough to believe that Arabella was an innocent party, concerned only for her welfare. 'Why bother? It just draws attention to their childish behaviour. Sometimes if you pay attention to negative behaviour, that's all you get.'

'You are so right, of course,' Arabella said, and Grace gave a little start as she felt Arabella put her arm through hers. She wanted to shove her away, but since she had no idea what Arabella was up to she thought better of it. 'But I still think you should tell someone. Bullying isn't tolerated at Henry Tyndale, you know.'

Arabella sounded every inch the prim and proper private school girl. Grace wanted to stand up and tell her exactly what she thought of her, but instead she said, 'I understand, but I'm fine, thank you.' She was surprised that she managed to unclench her jaw to say the words. What she really wanted was to speak to Adam, to see if he had any explanation at all for what was going on.

It was a great relief when the bell sound for the end of the lesson. Arabella turned her attention to her Barnacles, and Grace was able to make a quick exit. The corridor outside was full of students, both juniors and seniors. Grace wondered if she had finally given in to paranoia when some of the younger students started to point at her and giggle. Others just stared or whispered to their companions. As Grace made her way down the corridor, she came to the history notice board, all the notices completely obscured by copies of the caricature that Arabella had taken pains to show her. She stopped for a moment and then lifted a shaking hand to pull them down, one by one.

With her head down and a bundle of scrunched-up paper in her hand, she fled down the corridor to the stairs. The further she went from her classroom, the worse it got. The posters were everywhere, covering every notice board, stuck to every door. There was no way she could remove them all and she knew there was no point in trying. She dug her nails into the palms of each hand to try and stop the tears that were threatening to flow. When she reached the wide hall wall at the main entrance, it felt like safety was in her reach — just a few more steps and she would be at the stairs that would take her to her room.

7

'Miss Taylor.'

Grace stopped. All she wanted to do was get away, but she knew that she couldn't. She took a moment to try to compose her face, then turned around. The head of her year group, Mrs Bilton, was standing there looking concerned. Beside her was Arabella, doing an equally good impression of a person who cared. Behind them, at the end of the corridor, Grace could see Adam. She caught his eye and wished she could speak with him, to ask him if he knew what game was being played.

'Miss Taylor, please come with me.'

Grace swallowed hard and fell into step behind the tall, imposing figure of Mrs Bilton. She liked Mrs Bilton, who was very much a 'what you see is what you get' person, and Grace thought she was the teacher most likely to see through Arabella's mind games.

Mrs Bilton opened the door to her office. 'Arabella, please give us a moment. I would like to speak to you, too, so take a seat and I will call you shortly.' Then she turned to Grace. 'Please sit, my dear. Would you like a cup of tea? I appreciate that you must be upset.'

Grace nodded and watched as Mrs Bilton busied herself preparing the tea.

'I know that it can be very difficult being a scholarship girl at our school.' Grace nodded. 'Teenagers can represent the best and worst of humankind, and there seems little we can do to change it.'

Grace didn't agree. Although she wasn't sure what they could do, she felt they should do *something*.

'Do you know who drew the image?' Mrs Bilton spoke as if she had chosen the last word very carefully.

Grace swallowed a mouthful of tea to give her time to think. 'Not for sure, but I can take a guess.'

Mrs Bilton nodded. 'Arabella came to see me, as she was concerned for you. She says that you keep yourself to yourself, and she's worried that you are lonely and unhappy.'

Grace couldn't help it — a bite of sharp laughter left her and she raised a hand to her lips. She could feel Mrs Bilton watching her closely.

'I may be alone in this, Grace, but I appear to be immune to Arabella's charm.'

Grace stared and felt hope rise inside her.

'However — ' The very word made the hope die as if water had been thrown onto a fire. ' — without concrete proof there is little I can do, you understand? Arabella's father is represented on the board of governors and is a very influential man.'

This was not news to Grace, so she nodded.

'From one former scholarship girl to another, please can I ask you to be careful? In an ideal world I would be able to deal with Arabella, simply based on my instinct that behind the beautiful exterior lies a bully and a liar. But we do not live in an ideal world, Grace.' Mrs Bilton reached out and squeezed her arm, her face serious. 'I will invite her in and see what she has to say. Would you like to stay?'

'Yes,' Grace said, and for the first time she raised her head and looked Mrs Bilton straight in the eye.

Mrs Bilton opened the door and gestured for Arabella to take a seat beside Grace, then went to sit behind her desk. 'This, I think we can agree, has been a most hateful incident. And as you know, Arabella, we do not tolerate bullying in this school.'

Arabella nodded and then leaned forward. 'That's why I came to tell you, Mrs Bilton. I tried to persuade Grace to come and speak to you herself, although I completely understand why she didn't want to. Sometimes reporting things like this can make life so much worse, which is why I decided that Grace needed someone to stand up for her.'

Grace's eyes flicked to Mrs Bilton as she wondered if the teacher was being taken in, though a slight tightness around her eyes made Grace feel sure she wasn't.

Arabella seemed oblivious that her act was not working. 'Also, Mrs Bilton . . . ' Arabella looked down and began to wring her hands in her lap. She really was quite the actress. ' . . . I think I know who it might be.'

'Really,' Mrs Bilton said. 'And?'

There was a moment of dramatic silence. 'It's difficult, you see. She is a friend of mine.' Arabella made her eyes go wide, as if this were a terrible moral decision for her. 'But I can't just let her behave this way. I won't be friends with a bully.'

'That's good to hear, Arabella.' Mrs Bilton's tone was neutral. 'So perhaps you can tell me who I need to speak with next.'

'Camille. Camille De Frey.' Arabella maintained her gaze without a waver, and after a few moments Mrs Bilton nodded.

'Thank you, Arabella, for your honesty. Please find Camille and tell her I need to speak with her immediately.' Arabella nodded and stood up as if she were waiting for Grace. 'Then please return to your lesson. I have excused Grace for the rest of the day.'

Arabella turned and smiled sadly at Grace. 'I'm sorry this happened to you, Grace. Please know that you're always welcome to sit with me and my friends if you ever feel like some company.' She turned and smiled at Mrs Bilton. 'Don't worry — I will look out for Grace, Mrs Bilton.'

'I'm sure you will,' Mrs Bilton answered. Arabella left the room, and she said to Grace: 'I will of course punish Camille in line with the school policy on bullying. I'll make a note on her record, so if there are any further incidents please come straight to me.'

'Thank you,' Grace said before placing her now-empty teacup on the desk.

'I doubt she was alone in this, and in

fact I would be very surprised if it was her idea. I don't think Camille has had an independent thought since she arrived.'

Despite everything, Grace smiled.

'I'm sorry I can't do more for you, my dear. My door is always open if you need to talk. Can I suggest that you go and do some extra music practice?'

'I will, and thank you.'

* * *

Grace was halfway through her first piece when the door was pushed open with such force that it rebounded off of the wall with a loud crash. Startled, she looked up. Adam was standing in the doorway looking beside himself.

'There you are!' he said, crossing the room in three quick strides. 'I've been looking for you everywhere.'

'You didn't look in the most obvious place, then,' Grace answered, somehow unable to keep the amusement from her voice at the heart-warming thought that he had been looking for her.

Good point, well made,' he said with a small grin. 'You aren't usually here so early, though.' His voice had changed to once of concern.

'Mrs Bilton let me out of religious studies because of . . . well, you know.' She looked away then, feeling embarrassment grow again.

'It's all over the school.'

Grace frowned at his insensitive comment. 'I know; I saw,' she said dully. She felt him take her free hand.

'No, not that — although I suppose that is, too. No, Mrs Bilton hauled Camille De Frey out of class. Apparently you could hear her yelling all the way to the library.'

'Poor Camille,' Grace said, and was surprised to find that she meant it.

'You're feeling sorry for Camille?' Adam was incredulous. 'She's a mini-bitch who does whatever Arabella tells her to.'

Grace managed to smile a little at the vehemence in his voice. She shrugged.

'She's probably as much a victim as anyone.'

They stood and stared at each other, and Grace felt like an ocean had sprung up between them. She had always felt that Adam understood her, but now she wasn't sure of anything. Surely he could see that the Barnacles were desperate to fit in, which in itself was kind of sad. She watched Adam as he searched for something to say.

'And I bet you think Arabella is just misunderstood,' he eventually said with derision.

Grace laughed now. 'I wouldn't go that far.' She walked over and plonked herself down on the pile of old costumes that they used as a sofa. 'I've been giving it a lot of thought.'

'I don't think I could be that forgiving.'

'If you think about it, Camille is desperate to fit in; so desperate, in fact, that she was prepared to do something that she knew could get her into serious trouble. I'm sure she only did it because Arabella told her to. For all we know, Arabella promised her she wouldn't get into trouble.'

'So what you're saying is, basically she's too dumb to see when she's being used?' Adam said sceptically.

'I don't think she's dumb; I just think she's too afraid to stand up to Arabella. And I can't say I blame her. Being in Arabella's crosshairs is not pleasant.'

Adam moved now and settled into the 'sofa' beside her. 'I got Seb and his mates to take down all the drawings and get rid of them. They're pretty thorough, so they should all be gone.'

'Thanks,' Grace said, although deep down she wished that Adam had taken them down himself.

'I had no idea what she was planning,' he said, running a hand through his hair and making it stand up at odd angles. 'What did Mrs Bilton say to you?'

Grace shrugged. 'Not much. She, at least, sees through Arabella's innocent girl act; but there isn't much she can do without evidence.'

'Arabella's dad is too bloody rich, that's the problem! Not one of the teachers would dare to give her a punishment, in case he decides to stop funding the next big building project. I hate this place.' He punched the ground with his fist. 'I wish there was something I could do.'

He looked at Grace and she tried to smile. Inside she was shouting, *But there is! Tell Arabella that you and me are together! She might come after us, but at least we're together.* But instead she said, 'There isn't anything. You were right in your note. If we go public then it will be worse for both of us.' However, she silently willed him not to agree with her.

Adam sighed deeply. 'I suppose trying to fix hundreds of years of inbuilt snobbery and power is probably a bit out of our reach.' He jumped up and hauled Grace to her feet. 'Well, if we can't fix it, then we should stop talking about it. You should be practising and I should be listening, hanging on to every note and showering you with praise!'

Despite the sharp disappointment she felt inside, Grace couldn't help but be a little won over by Adam's enthusiasm, though she wished she could push aside the pain as easily. He was right — she should be practising; and at least his presence was a comfort. She picked up her violin and played.

She was on the final bars of the piece when Adam's watch beeped, and she lifted her bow away from the strings. Adam looked at her, and his face was easy to read: he had to go but he wanted to stay. Grace managed a smile. Music as always had been a great tonic, and she felt better despite the awful events of the day. It had helped, of course, that Adam had sat and watched her play, giving her his full attention. She doubted that he could have sat still for so long if he had not genuinely wanted to be there.

She watched as he walked towards her and her heart flipped; she wondered if he would kiss her. Carefully he took the violin and bow from her hands and set them on the piano. Then he took each of her hands in his, and she could not take her eyes away from his face.

'I'll find out what Arabella's up to,' he said, 'and I promise you I'll stop it. I won't let today happen again, ever.'

Grace smiled, but Adam could read the uncertainty on her face. She knew that he meant his words; she just doubted he would be able to follow through.

'I promise, Gracie. Trust me.' He leaned in then, and Grace's breath caught in her throat. His eyes were watchful, as if he expected her to tell him to leave her alone. But all she wanted in that moment was to be kissed, and to feel safe and loved, so she leaned in too. The kiss was delicate and sweet, as if they had all the time in the world. They were so in synch that they both reluctantly drew away at the same time.

'I have to go.'

'You have to go.' They smiled at the unison of their words.

'I'll try to come back to see you later, but it depends how Seb is.'

Grace nodded her understanding. 'I'll be waiting.'

He lifted her hand to his lips and kissed it. Grace was reminded of knights and ladies of long ago, and now she knew what people meant when they said their hearts fluttered. Adam bowed and then walked swiftly to the door. When he reached it, he turned and nodded one final time before he left. Grace put her hand to her heart, feeling like she needed to do something to keep it in her chest, and allowed herself a moment to replay the kiss, as well as his touch and the sensations that came with it.

A cold voice with a slight accent broke through Grace's reverie. 'I wondered what Adam was doing in here.' She did not need to look to see who the owner of the voice was. She turned her head away to give herself a moment to calm down, dreading what was coming next.

8

'Do you need the room for music practice?' Grace asked evenly, despite the fact that she knew that Arabella did not play an instrument and would never dream of attempting to take on something so unworthy of her time.

Arabella raised a contemptuous eyebrow, which clearly gave the message 'as if'. She stepped into the room and closed the door, then stood in front of it. Grace understood the implied threat in the action but chose to ignore it.

'Well in that case, I need to practise.' Grace moved and picked up her violin, lifting it to her chin. Arabella crossed the distance between them in short steps and wrenched the violin from Grace's arm, tearing one of the strings from its peg as she did so. Grace knew better than to respond to this; if she did, she suspected that her violin would be thrown across the room.

Arabella practically snarled, 'Stay away from Adam. He's too good for you.'

Grace took a step backwards. She had no idea how Arabella had found out their secret.

'Adam is mine. He belongs to me. We're a perfect fit. I have no idea what you think you're doing, but you need to stop it right now.' She plucked at one of the remaining strings of the violin, looking from Grace to the instrument with a sort of bored intention.

Grace reached out a hand. 'Please, give it back.'

'Why should I? You've taken something of mine, so it seems only right that I take something of yours.'

Grace swallowed. 'Adam doesn't belong to anyone, so maybe you need to have this conversation with him.'

Arabella tilted her head to one side. 'You're nothing to him you, know. Just a distraction. Boys are so like that when a new toy comes along. They play with it for a while but they soon get bored.

And he *will* get bored — but that's not the worst thing that'll happen.' She paused now, and Grace knew she was supposed to ask what that thing was. She also knew that she could not risk her violin.

'What?' she asked. Her voice, even to her own ears, sounded small.

'I can make your life miserable.'

Grace wanted to answer that she was already managing that. The two things that made her life bearable at Tyndale were her music and Adam. She felt coldness grow in the pit of her stomach and knew she would have to choose.

'It would be such a shame if the charity girl's instruments were damaged in some way. I'm guessing that your *folks* — ' She said the word with such distain that Grace had to fight the urge to lash out. ' — probably can't afford to buy you new ones, or even second-hand ones.' Grace watched as Arabella turned over her violin and studied it. 'I'm guessing it would be hard to maintain your scholarship with no instruments to play. We're not a state school, you know; we don't have instruments lying around so poor people can play them. Tyndale expects that you'll at least be able to provide your own. Of course.'

The choice was there. Arabella had not said it in so many words, but Grace did not doubt her intention. If she did not agree to give up Adam, Arabella would find a way — a way that did not lead back to her — to destroy Grace's instruments, and therefore her dreams.

'Of course, that would just be the beginning,' Arabella continued. 'You charity girls have to maintain academic standards as well, so imagine how difficult that'd be for you if I made sure you couldn't access the library or the computer hall.'

Grace wanted to call her bluff — to tell her that she would not be threatened; that she would tell someone. Mrs Bilton would know that Arabella's threats were potentially criminal. But she knew it was hopeless. No one would believe the new girl over the most popular girl at school, who had a legion of other students under her sway to follow her commands to the letter. Mrs Bilton's words reverberated around her head: 'Without proof, there is little I can do.' And of course Grace had no proof. Arabella was smart, and there was no way that Grace would be able to prove that this conversation had even occurred. Arabella probably had a crowd of other students ready to swear that she had been with them the whole time and hadn't gone near the music practice rooms. Grace would be labelled a liar, and no doubt Arabella would claim that Grace was in fact bullying her!

'What is it that you want me to do?' Grace asked quietly, knowing the answer but needing to hear it.

'I don't want you to *do* anything. This is more about what I want you to *stop* doing.'

Grace nodded, feeling ashamed that she had to give in to this mean, spoilt girl, but knowing that she had no real choice.

'Stop seeing Adam. It's simple, really.

If he needs encouragement to stop seeing you, then I expect you to do something about it.' Grace nodded and Arabella held out her violin. Grace reached for it but Arabella did not loosen her grip. 'Of course I expect you to leave my name out of this, or . . . ' She left the rest unsaid.

Grace felt a flash of anger. It was hardly an agreement, but she forced her feelings down and nodded.

'And don't even think about running to a teacher, especially Mrs Bilton.'

Grace nodded again, forcing herself not to give in to tears.

'And in case you need more incentive, don't forget that Adam's father would do anything to protect him.'

'Protect him from what?' Grace knew that her contribution was unnecessary, but she couldn't help herself.

'From girls like you. Girls from poor backgrounds who work hard to worm their way into the lives of rich boys with bright futures. Girls who trap boys for their own ends. If Adam's father was to find about you, then who knows what he'd do. Maybe send Adam to another school, away from Seb. My father and his father are very close friends. It wouldn't just be your own future you'd be damaging. And I'd hate to see how Seb would cope on his own.'

Grace was determined not to let Arabella see her cry. Arabella studied her for a moment and then released her hold on the instrument. Grace cradled the violin to herself.

'Then I suggest you get on with your practice. We wouldn't want you to get thrown off of your musical scholarship, now, would we?'

★ ★ ★

Grace watched as Arabella walked away from her, holding in all her anger and frustration. As Arabella stepped outside she turned and smiled, a perfect imitation of a nice girl that she turned on teachers at every opportunity. 'So nice that we could have a little chat. I almost feel like we're friends.' She shook out her perfectly groomed hair, smiled and left.

Grace was shaking with anger and pain. She felt for the piano stool and sat down heavily, then reached for her violin case and pulled out a new string, making her hands and head focus on the task of restringing. Her mind felt at war with itself. How could she have let this happen? How could she have let herself be bullied to this extent — to let some vacuous girl have such control over her life? She knew the answer, of course. She was effectively in enemy territory, and Arabella had all the power and influence. Grace had no doubt that Arabella could work her magic and force her from the school, most likely in disgrace, and then all her musical dreams would be gone. But then there was Adam, and those feelings that were so new and exciting, and she knew she could not let him be hurt either. Her feelings for Adam were real, and after that evening she was sure he felt the same.

She packed up her instruments and fled back to the relative safety of her room. Adam would not come looking for her there, as boys were forbidden on the girls' dormitory floor. That would at least give her the rest of the evening and the night to figure just what she was going to do.

★ ★ ★

Grace was tired but could not sleep. Her mind refused to be quiet, and instead replayed the events of the evening. She realised that whatever she did, she would lose Adam. If she chose to ignore Arabella's threats, then she was in no doubt that her time at the school would be short; she would, for some reason or other, be sent home. It was unlikely that her fledgling relationship with Adam, if that was what it was, could survive her being sent away, or him being sent away from Seb.

The bell sounded to tell her that it was time to get up. She knew what she had to do, and she knew that she did not have a choice. Or rather, the choice was whether or not to lose her musical dream; she had already lost Adam the moment Arabella had stepped into the practice room. Now all she needed to do was convince him that whatever they had was over, if it had ever even started.

After classes finished for the day, Grace decided to skip supper. She had kept her head down all day; and Adam, for his part, seemed to be giving all his attention to Arabella, who was revelling in it. Grace remembered his words from the night before and wondered if it was all just an act to find out what Arabella was up to. Not that it mattered anymore. Grace headed straight for her practice room and drew across the sign that said it was occupied.

She tried again to rehearse what she would say to Adam; what she would need to say to make him leave her alone. She hoped that a simple rebuff would be enough, as teenage boys were generally quite sensitive about rejection.

She hoped that it would be as quick and painless as possible — painless for him, at least, though not for her. Their short acquaintance had all been a fantasy, one that she had indulged for far too long to be good for her, Grace told herself. She forced down the feelings of anger and shame before they could break through her carefully constructed wall. Her life had been full before Adam, and it would be again; all she needed was a little time to settle back into her life as it was. She needed to find that single-minded focus on the Royal College of Music that had sustained her for so long.

After sitting down at the piano, she put the latest piece she was learning on the stand. It had a tragic air to it, and after the first page she forced herself to stop. This was definitely not helping. Instead she dived in to her music bag and pulled out an Irish jig that was her father's favourite.

'Somehow I doubt that's a Tyndale approved piece.'

She heard Adam jump down from the stage and walk towards the piano. His footsteps told her he was doing a mocking dance. She stopped and stared at him coldly. 'It's my dad's favourite.' She was shocked by the coldness in her voice, but she had practised it.

'Okay, I can see why he might like it.' Adam smiled.

'What's that supposed to mean?'

'That I like it, too?' He finished the statement with a question mark. 'Are you okay?' He looked concerned now, and it was all Grace could do to hold back what she was truly feeling. She wanted to tell him about Arabella and her threats but knew that she couldn't. She wasn't sure how he would react, but she figured that anger would feature. She allowed herself a moment to imagine Adam calling Arabella out on her threats, and reporting her to the head, to his father. Then she herself could stay and be with Adam. But then an alternative ending to the fairy tale floated before her — one where she ruined Adam's life, Adam's father accused her of leading his son astray, she was sent home in disgrace, and all her dreams were ruined. One where Adam and Seb were separated.

'I need to practise,' she said flatly.

Adam smiled, but Grace could detect a slight hint of uncertainty. 'Of course. I'll sit here and listen — your biggest fan, as always.' He made a deep bow and then moved towards the piano. He went to sit beside her on the stool, but she turned her face away.

'If you don't want an audience, I can leave.'

'I *don't* want an audience. I need to focus on my music.'

He edged around the piano so that he could see her face. 'Are you saying I'm a distraction?' His voice was playful now.

'Yes,' Grace answered. Again, her voice was flat.

'Gracie, what's wrong? Is it Arabella? Today was just about trying to find out what she was up to, you know that.'

'Do I?' Grace said, looking up for the first time.

'Yes,' he answered rather defensively. 'We talked about this yesterday. In order to protect you, I need to — '

'As I remember it, you talked and I agreed like a brainless idiot. Today you just looked like you always do, to me: part of the in crowd, flirting with Arabella, lapping up all the attention. Ignoring me. Well I've had enough of your games, Adam. I came to this school with only one goal, to win a place at the Royal College, and that's what I intend to do. Nothing else matters.' The last sentence tasted like charcoal on her lips.

'And here I was thinking that you were different. That you were brave enough to stand up to the falseness of this place.' He waved his arms in frustration. 'But you're just like everyone else. I never thought you'd be one to give in so easily, Grace.'

Grace's mind raged. So easily? How could he say that? He had no idea what life had been like for her. He had said he understood, but he clearly didn't. She knew that he was hurt and angry; but somehow, in a small way, he was making it easier for her.

'It was all just pretend, don't you see? We thought we could change this place but we can't. You can't change who you are, and neither can I. I didn't come to this school to meet a rich boy; I came because it's the best chance I have of following my dream. Since you came into this room, my life's been more difficult, and every day it gets harder to stay focused on what I really want.' Grace felt breathless when she finished. She could hardly look at Adam.

His eyes narrowed and his face became blank. 'Fine. Whatever. I'll go back to being me, and you can be miserable on your own.' With that, he turned swiftly and walked to the door. 'But, Grace — don't expect me to come to your rescue again. You ended this, so it's gone, forgotten.' He walked out and let the door slam behind him.

9

If Grace had thought that following Arabella's instructions would make life better for her, then she was mistaken. Arabella continued as if nothing had happened between them. When the mood took her, she was a bully, the rest of the time she acted as if Grace did not exist. Grace tried to tell herself this was fine; it was only what she could expect Arabella to do. But it still hurt, particularly when Arabella and the Barnacles were in a vicious mood.

But Grace knew the real source of her own pain. Adam had been true to his word; he never came to her rescue. Occasionally Grace thought he looked uncomfortable when Arabella was picking on her, but the look was fleeting, and he would never meet her eye. There were times when she blamed him, and questioned whether their brief relationship had even been real. If it was, why hadn't he put up more of a fight when she'd rejected him — didn't it occur to him that she'd had a good reason? Why could he not see that Arabella was behind it? But at other times, Grace felt sure she could see how unhappy Adam was. He was the top dog, but didn't seem to revel in it. It was like he was going through the motions, and doing what was expected of him by his father and the other students who worshipped him as their leader.

Grace now focused on her music and lived for playing. The weeks passed, and Christmas came round more quickly than she would have thought possible. The two weeks she spent at home were wonderful. There she could be herself and relax, rather than having to watch out for when the next attack might come.

But back at school, nothing had changed, not even 'her' music practice room. Grace's parents had brought her a cello case on wheels as a Christmas present, which made it much easier to transport the instrument. Upon her return after the holidays, she pushed it into the practice room in front of her, then bent down to open it — when suddenly she had a sense that she was not alone. She stood quickly and tensed, alert for what might come next. Scanning the room, she could see no sign of anyone — but that did not mean that Arabella or one of her cronies was not there.

'Who's there?' she called out, trying to keep her nerves steady.

There was a rustling from the stage, and Adam stepped out from behind the crumpled curtains. 'Don't look so worried. It's just me.' He jumped off the stage. 'I just needed to escape for a while, but I'll leave.'

Grace looked at him. Now that he'd come closer, she could see he looked tired. He had dark circles under his eyes, and it seemed like the effort of standing up was almost too much for him. 'Are you okay?' She knew she shouldn't ask, and should just let him go, but he looked so wretched she just couldn't. She took a step towards him and he backed away.

'Adam?' she asked.

'Seb's sick.' His voice sounded strangled, and Grace suspected he was trying to hold his feelings in. 'Really sick.'

Grace could stand it no longer. She crossed the distance between them and pulled Adam into her arms. He resisted at first, like he did not want to give in; but finally he crumbled, and she could feel him shake in her arms as he cried. She rubbed his back and held him, not knowing what else to do or say.

'I'm sorry,' he sniffed. 'I shouldn't have come. I know things aren't the same between us. It's just . . . all through Christmas I kept thinking that if I could just talk to you, it'd be better.' He ran his hand through his hair, looking lost. 'Seb got really sick on Christmas Eve. His chest is bad. They say it's pneumonia, and we aren't sure if he is going to . . . ' His voice cracked.

'There isn't anyone else I can talk to; no one who can understand. My parents are distraught, and the people here aren't exactly understanding of anyone's feelings.'

'You can talk to me,' Grace said quietly. 'You can always talk to me.' She took him by the hand and led him to the pile of clothes that served as a sofa. They sat next to each other and Grace waited for him to speak.

'I didn't want to come back,' Adam said quietly. 'My father made me. He said there was nothing I could do for Seb, and that it'd be better for my mother if she wasn't worried about me too. He said the best thing I could do for all of them was to focus on my studies.' He shook his head violently. 'As if I care about exams!'

'I'm sorry.' Grace squeezed his hand. 'That must be tough.'

'I told Seb I'd always be there, you know? I'm his big brother, and I can't bear the thought of him being there alone.'

'Your parents are with him,' Grace said gently.

'But what if something happens? What if he gets worse and there's no time for me to . . . ' He rubbed at his eyes fiercely now, seeming determined not to allow the tears to flow.

'I'm sure they'll call if something changes. Seb is amazing; he might well surprise you.'

'He isn't supposed to have made it this far. When he was a baby ne nearly died four times. He *is* pretty incredible.' Adam seemed lost in his thoughts, so Grace just sat there beside him.

'Thank you,' he said after the silence. 'I know you want me to believe what you said, but I know you're different, really; not like the others.'

Grace felt the all-too-familiar sharp pain in her chest and for a moment wanted to tell him everything, but knew that she shouldn't. Adam was already in meltdown, and she had no idea how he would react to the news of what Arabella had done. If she truly cared about him, she needed to protect him from that. So she gave a noncommittal shrug. 'If you need to talk about Seb, or you want to escape for a bit, then my door is always open, so to speak.'

Adam laughed and Grace was grateful to see him lifted a little. 'I wouldn't mind hearing you play sometimes,' he said. 'I won't distract you.'

Grace doubted he knew how untrue that last sentence was. His very presence, even when he was silent and attentive, was a distraction. But she couldn't bring herself to turn him away, not when he had so much to deal with.

'You know where I am,' she said, and watched as he left the room, her mind in turmoil.

10

Grace kept a close eye on Adam over the next few weeks. He had been in the music practice room a few times after their initial post-Christmas meeting, and continued to look worn-out and pale. She had not needed to ask him how Seb was, as his greeting each time was 'no change' before he would collapse on the old costume sofa and listen to her play in silence. He was not his usual self outside of the practice room, either. Despite the best efforts of Arabella and his mates, he remained on the periphery of their activities, only taking part when he had to.

Arabella was attentive and sympathetic, and Adam allowed her to be, although Grace felt sure that she could see he took no comfort from her ministrations. Not that it should matter if he did. She knew she had hurt him with her rejection, and felt sure he would remember that as soon as Seb was on the mend. Although she didn't relish the thought of losing him again, she could not bring herself to wish anything other than Sebastian's full recovery.

One cold February day, Grace was already up before the morning bell — as was her habit now to avoid the Barnacles — and was making her way to the practice room. If she rushed her breakfast, she could squeeze in an extra thirty minutes of practice, and she felt like she needed it. She relished the challenges of new music, but her studies seemed to take up more and more of her time. She had been up late finishing her maths homework, which was also important, as her scholarship required academic as well as musical excellence.

This was what she was focused on as she hurried down the last few stairs from the girls' floor. Not paying attention to where she was going, she crashed into something solid. Her sheet music case opened as it fell, and the floor was awash with it in moments.

'Sorry! My fault; not watching where I was . . . ' Her voice trailed off as she realised that she had run full-pelt into Adam. 'Oh,' was all she could think to say before she dropped to her knees and started to collect the sheets.

'Here, let me help you,' he said, kneeling beside her. He reached out for a sheet and their hands brushed. Grace felt that electric shock sensation that she had only ever felt from touching him. She allowed herself to look at him and realised that he had felt it too. He seemed frozen in place. She threw a quick glance around the wide entrance hall, hoping that no one had seen them. It was silent and still and she let out her held-in breath.

'How's Seb?' she asked.

Adam stood and handed her the last few sheets. 'The same, really. I'm working on my father, though, like you said — trying to convince him to let me visit. Mostly I want to just quit school and turn up there; but knowing my father, he still wouldn't let me see him. So I decided to follow your advice.'

Grace wished for the hundredth time that Arabella did not exist. She wanted to be there for Adam — to be his friend, every day for every moment — but a small voice was warning her in her head. She needed to leave the entrance hall now, before someone saw them. Arabella had eyes and ears everywhere. 'I'm sure your dad will see reason and let you see Seb soon,' she said, trying to inject some hopefulness into her voice.

'You don't know my father.'

Grace wanted to stay, to keep him company and find a way to relieve some of his pain, but she knew she couldn't. 'I have to go, but I'll be practising as usual tonight.' Without waiting for a reply, she fled, trying to fight back the confusing mix of anger and shame she felt every time she thought about how she was letting Arabella dictate her life.

The day did not improve: the maths homework she had spent so many hours working on had a fundamental flaw, and she needed to start all over again. This was in addition to all the extra work she had been set throughout the day, which made for a tough choice. As much as she hated the thought, she needed to skip her usual evening music practice. Her maths teacher had given her a pretty straightforward ultimatum: either get her work up to scratch, or risk failing, which in turn could jeopardise her scholarship.

Grace knew it would be another late night trying to get two sets of homework done. The worst thing, which she hated to admit even to herself, was the fact that she wouldn't get to see Adam. She had tried giving herself a stern talking-to about the dangers of getting too comfortable with him, and of giving him the wrong impression, but somehow she couldn't stop her growing feelings for him. Maybe a night away from the practice room would do her good. She just wished she could get a message to Adam to tell him why she would not be there.

She was sitting in her last class of the day, doing her best to concentrate and fight back the yawns that were ever-threatening. Arabella seemed to be focused on another girl in their year and acted as if Grace did not exist. Grace was ashamed to admit to herself that she was glad someone else was the target today, as she did not feel she had the energy to take the abuse.

The classroom door opened and Mr McKenzie, head of the upper school, entered the room. 'Please excuse my interruption Mrs Yardley, but I need to speak with Miss Taylor,' he said.

Grace looked up in shock at the mention of her name and stood up, her chair making a scraping noise on the floor. She could feel the stares of everyone else in the class and was sure that Arabella was laughing at her. She could not see Adam, who was sitting behind her, but she could feel his concern — or perhaps she was imagining it.

'Bring your things, Miss Taylor. You will not be returning to class today.'

Grace's heart lurched, and she immediately thought that something terrible had happened to her parents. With shaking hands, she shoved her books and pens into her bag and hurried out of the classroom after her teacher. Mr McKenzie was silent as he marched along the corridors, past classrooms full of students, and this only made Grace's fears grow. She wanted to ask what had happened, but felt sure he would say nothing until they reached his office. Once inside, she waited expectantly.

'Take a seat, Miss Taylor. I need to speak with you about a matter of grave concern.'

Grace's voice dried up in her throat and she nodded. Mr McKenzie reached for a sheaf of papers on his desk and handed them to her.

'Is this your homework, Miss Taylor?'

Grace blinked in surprise and then took the sheets from him. 'Yes,' she answered, the confusion evident in her voice.

'Did anyone assist you with this piece of work?'

She looked up now and found that Mr McKenzie was examining her closely. 'No. Well, Miss Truss went through it with me so that I understood where I went wrong.' She could not work out what was going on.

'Do you recognise this?' He handed her another piece of paper. This one was in different handwriting. The name at the top said 'Melissa Robinson'. Grace felt coldness start in the pit of her stomach. Melissa was a wannabe-Barnacle in her maths set. She swallowed the lump in her throat and forced herself to appear calm, even though inside she felt deep suspicion that she knew what was coming next.

'This is Melissa's homework, sir. I've not seen it before.' She saw doubt in his eyes and knew that he didn't believe her.

'Then perhaps you can explain to me why you have all the same correct answers as well as the workings-out? Both pieces of work are identical.'

'Melissa must have copied my work,'

Grace said. Her voice sounded small even to her own ears.

Mr McKenzie raised an eyebrow. 'I have spoken to Miss Truss, and she tells me that Melissa's work is of a consistently high standard, whereas yours has been somewhat lacking.'

'I spent all of last night in library working on it! I even skipped my music practice.'

'Miss Taylor, whilst I sympathise with the difficulties students can experience when transferring from state schools to a school such as Henry Tyndale, we cannot overlook this serious breach of school rules. Copying another student's work is not tolerated, whatever the circumstances. To do so without that student's knowledge — therefore risking their academic record and reputation — raises questions around your moral aptitude.'

Grace clenched her hands in her lap as the anger hit her full-force. How dare he question her morals! The whole school was a lie. The popular students got away with murder whilst the others were mercilessly bullied, and no teacher ever took any action to prevent it.

'I completed my homework by myself with no help from anyone. I am not a cheat.' The last sentence came out through gritted teeth.

'Then how do you explain the fact that your work is identical to Miss Robinson's?'

'Melissa must have copied my work. It's the only explanation.'

'And why would she do that?'

Grace knew she had lost this battle before it had even started; Mr McKenzie had made up his mind. But she was still compelled to tell him the truth. 'Maybe to get me into trouble.' She made herself look him squarely in the eye.

'To get you into trouble? And why would Miss Robinson want to get you into trouble?'

'Because she wants to be friends with Arabella and her gang, and this would be a good way of getting in her good books. Arabella hates me and would do anything to get me into trouble. She wants me sent home in disgrace!'

'Miss Taylor, I must stop you there. Defending your dishonest behaviour by creating a fabricated story where you are the victim, and calling yet more of our fine students' behaviour into question, is not to be tolerated. I will be calling your parents so that they are present at your disciplinary meeting, which will be at ten o'clock tomorrow morning. I don't need to tell you how seriously the school takes behaviour such as yours.'

Grace stood up, desperate to escape Mr McKenzie's judgement. She wanted to say more, but she knew there was no point; no one would believe her or even listen to her. It was over, and Arabella had won.

'Miss Taylor.' Mr McKenzie's voice demanded her attention and she turned. 'I don't think I need to remind you that your scholarship place is now in grave jeopardy.'

Grace said nothing; she couldn't find any words at all. She opened the door and fled down the corridor.

11

She escaped to the one place that she felt safe: her music room. 'Adam?' she asked softly, hoping he was there waiting for her. But her question was answered with silence. She was alone.

She tried to practise her music, but she couldn't seem to make her fingers respond, and her heart felt as if it had stopped. She needed to see Adam. Her mind went to her parents, who had no doubt been called by now. She knew they would believe her, but she doubted there was much they could do. Grace had no way of proving her innocence; no way of proving that Arabella was behind all of this. Her heart tightened at the thought of the upset she would cause her parents. Why hadn't she just stayed away from Adam? She knew the answer, but right now she couldn't help wondering if she had made the right decision.

The door opened and Grace looked up, feeling both frightened and relieved that Adam had finally come for her. He stepped into the room but wouldn't look at her. She crossed the room quickly, needing him to say something; to say he believed her. When she was inches away from him, he looked up, and the expression on his face made her pause.

'Adam?'

'It's Seb,' was all he managed before he fell towards her, and she encircled him in her arms. She felt her own tears come now and she didn't try to stop them. The thought of Seb, funny and sweet but so unwell or maybe worse, made her sobs come more quickly, and were mirrored by Adam's own. She wanted to know what happened but couldn't bring herself to ask, so she just held him tight.

'He's on a ventilator, in intensive care. His condition got worse and Father had to make a decision.'

Grace felt a faint glimmer of hope. At

least he was alive, then.

It was as if Adam sensed her thoughts. 'You don't understand,' he said, pulling back. 'His lungs are so damaged, they may never get him off it again. This could be it, Grace. Seb could die.' His face crumbled again but he remained where he was, his arms pulled tightly around himself. 'They've put him in a coma but he might never wake up. I'll never get to see him again. He'll think I didn't care enough to be there.'

Grace reached out for Adam's face and held it so that he was forced to look at her. 'Seb knows you love him, Adam. He worships you and he knows how much you care. You take care of him and look out for him. I not sure of much right now, but I know that for sure.' She took him by the hand and led him to their sofa. They collapsed into it together, arms wrapped tightly around each other.

'Father said he'd call and let me know. He sounded awful — he actually cried. I've never heard him cry before.'

Grace leaned up and kissed him. 'Everybody loves Seb. He's a great kid. He even looks out for me.'

Adam managed a smile. 'He's a good judge of people, and he liked you from the start; can't stop going on about you. I know how he feels,' he added, then looked away.

Grace wanted to tell him about Arabella, but she was afraid he would be angry with her, or with Arabella, and that he would lash out and do something he would later regret.

'I love you Gracie. You're the only good thing in my life at this school.' He sounded fierce.

'Adam, I . . . ' She wanted to pour it all out.

'I know you don't feel the same; that you want to concentrate on your music. But I needed to tell you.' He turned to her and kissed her gently, as if waiting for permission. All the sadness and pain that had welled up inside Grace were pushed aside by his touch.

'I love you, too,' she whispered, giving in to the kiss. Time seemed to still, and she felt as if she were caught in a beam of sunlight. Everything else faded in the bright hopefulness of the moment. But a thought made the light dim. 'What if you're father calls? No one knows where you are,' she said, drawing back from Adam a little.

'I told Camille. She said she'd come and find me.'

'Camille?' Grace couldn't keep the alarm in her voice.

'She came and spoke to me after class today, after Mr McKenzie pulled you out.'

Grace could feel his questioning gaze. 'None of that's important right now,' she said firmly, though the thought of the meeting the next day brought an intense flash of shame.

'It is important, Grace.'

She shook her head and tried to keep the pain from showing. 'Seb's important, and you are. The rest is just stuff to worry about tomorrow.'

'If Seb was at school, he'd say it was important. In fact, I wouldn't be able to stop him from marching into Mr McKenzie's office and demanding a full apology on your behalf.'

'I wish he was here,' Grace whispered, holding in a sob.

'Me too.'

They kissed again, and for a moment Grace wondered how much Camille had said; whether she had told Adam of Arabella's plans. His kisses felt certain, as if the past had been forgotten or at least explained. Grace felt Adam's hands caress her back and in turn she pulled him closer to her. Tomorrow her fate would be sealed; she would be leaving the school in disgrace. Her dreams of a place at the Royal College would be over; her academic transcripts would bear the permanent stain of cheating. Her tears flowed at the sense of injustice and loss. Adam drew back and, using his thumb, gently brushed away her tears.

'Tomorrow they'll send me home,' she said softly.

Adam shook his head. 'I'm going to go to Mr McKenzie and tell him about Arabella. About all of it.'

Grace saw the flash of anger that she'd feared. 'No, Adam. I don't think he'd believe you, and Arabella would find a way to hurt you too. She probably already has a plan. Your parents have enough to deal with; they can't cope with you being in trouble at school — or worse, getting kicked out. I won't let her hurt you, not over me.'

'Nothing can hurt me more than losing you and Seb. I should have done something before.'

'You won't lose me,' Grace said. 'You're the best thing about this place. Seb will get better. I'll go to college, and in a few years you'll be done with this place. I'll write; we'll keep in touch.'

'But what about the Royal College?'

'That dream was over the moment I was accused of cheating.'

Adam pulled away and stood up. His fists were clenched and his face set.

Grace got to her feet and held on to his arm.

'It's over, Adam. There's nothing you can do. Pease — I couldn't bear the thought of something happening to you to, to ruin your future too. We have tonight together and we can keep in touch; meet up in the holidays.' She looked at him closely now. It felt like the real test. Did she mean enough to him for him to let it go?

'I can't. I can't let this happen to you, Grace. It's not fair, and we can't let them win. This is all my fault; I should have stood up to her before. If our situations were reversed, you would've done this for me. I'm a coward. I don't care about this place, or my future.'

He raked his hand through his hair. Grace put an arm out to him, but he turned away, and before she could stop him his fist flew and he punched the wall. Then she put her arms around him. At first he resisted, but then gave in.

'So don't let them win,' she said.

'Don't let them steal your future, too, or put your parents through more hell than they're already going through. I'm going to go home and go to college, with my old friends. I'll be fine.' She tried to make her voice sound positive, but a deep pit had opened up inside her, full of shame and failure. All of her hard work and sacrifices had amounted to nothing in the face of a spiteful girl.

'I'm so sorry, Gracie.'

'It's not your fault. There are some things in the world that we just can't change.'

She stood on her tiptoes and kissed him. It was a determined kiss, full of passion and hope for an unknown future. He responded in kind, and Grace felt like she had captured the sunlight again. She would find a way to have music in her life, but right now all that mattered was her and Adam. When they broke apart, she felt like her breath was gone from her, and his was ragged too.

'I love you, Gracie.'

'I love you, too.'

Grace reached up a hand and rubbed away Adam's frown. Pulling his head down, she kissed him, and he kissed her back. She pushed away all the pain and the fear, and gave in to the moment, determined to savour the time they had together before the world intruded upon them again.

'Promise me you'll keep in touch,' Adam whispered.

'Only if you promise, too.'

They took a step back from each other.

'I promise,' they both said softly, and sealed it with a kiss.

The Present

1

'Could I have your autograph, please?'

Grace stopped walking but didn't turn around, sure she had imagined it.

'Miss Taylor, I'm a big fan. If you have a few minutes — ? I have a pen and a copy of the programme.'

Now Grace did turn slowly around, not sure what to expect. Standing before her was a tall young man in that age group between a child and a grown-up where you couldn't quite tell how old they were. She smiled to hide her surprise at having such a young, handsome fan.

'I'm sorry, I thought you must have been speaking to someone else. I've never been asked before.' She took the pen and the programme and wondered what you were supposed to write in moments like these.

'Can you dedicate it to me?' The

young man's voice was clear and confident, which surprised Grace, since most boys in their teens could barely manage to put two words together when speaking to an older woman.

'Of course. Like I said, not used to this. What's your name?' she asked before looking up and getting a good look at him for the first time. She felt a slight flash of recognition — more like an itch in her brain, and wondered if she had seen him somewhere before.

'Sebastian,' he said. 'But most of my friends call me Seb.'

Grace had written the 'S' and the 'e' before her brain finally connected the dots. For a heartbeat she just stared at her hands, wondering why they were shaking. It couldn't be! The last she had, heard Sebastian had been in intensive care on a ventilator and his prognosis had been bleak. That was eight years ago. Then she felt a hand touch her shoulder.

'Gracie, are you okay?'

She forced herself to swallow. 'Seb

— Sebastian?' Her eyes went wide with shock as her brain confirmed it. He was much taller, of course, but he looked strong and well. 'It can't be!' she said, and without thinking about what she was doing she drew him into a quick tight hug. Then she stepped back, holding him at arm's reach so that she could see him again. 'I thought . . . ' Her voice trailed off, as she didn't want to voice her worst fears.

'That I was dead?' Seb said laughing, reminding her so much of the cheeky nine-year-old she had met on her first day at Henry Tyndale. 'Let's just say reports of my death have been greatly exaggerated.'

Grace shook her head; she could not believe what she was seeing. After all these years, she had accepted that she would never know what happened to Seb, or to . . . She pushed his name firmly from her mind with ease due to years of practice.

'Perhaps we could go find somewhere to have coffee?' Seb suggested. 'We have a lot to catch up on.' He offered Grace his arm in an old-fashioned way and she took it. Part of her didn't want to find out what had happened in the past eight years; it was just too painful. But another part of her, a small part that time had not been able to extinguish, pushed her forward. After all, what harm could it do to spend time with her first boyfriend's little brother?

She found herself sitting at a table in the window of a coffee shop close to the Albert Hall. The November evening had a distinct chill to it, and she was glad to be indoors. She watched as Seb queued at the counter and collected their order, marvelling once again at the miracle he was.

'So, I'm still alive. How have you been?' Seb said, and Grace laughed once more. He really hadn't changed all that much.

'Oh no,' she said, shaking her head, 'you can't get away with that. All this time I thought that . . . well, the worst had happened — and here you are, all tall and healthy-looking. If you think you're going to get away without a proper explanation, you have another thing coming.' She smiled and took a sip of her milky coffee.

Seb shrugged. 'It's not much of a story. First I was sick, then I was *really* sick, and then I had a lung transplant.'

Grace gaped but somehow was not surprised that Seb had retained his general nonchalance about big events. 'Wow,' was all she could manage.

'Yep. Pretty impressive, I guess. Not so much for me, since all I did was lie there and trade one pair of worn-out lungs for a second-hand, barely used pair.'

Grace took a moment to take it all in. Although Seb's tone was light-hearted, she could detect a more solemn undertone. She nodded in understanding, wondering if he would say more.

'I was lucky; they found me a donor just at the right time.'

Grace reached out for his free hand and squeezed it as he took a sip of his coffee, giving him time to compose his answer.

'*I* was lucky, but not so good for my donor.'

'That's a pretty big thing to get your head around,' Grace said, not even able to imagine where to start.

'So my therapist tells me.' Seb's face relaxed and his youthful smile returned. 'Father insisted that when I dyed my hair blue, apparently I was showing signs of 'adjustment issues'.' He mimicked two inverted commas as he said it.

'Is it helping?' Grace asked, deciding to steer clear of the topic of Seb's father, which was too closely associated with the pain that she kept locked away.

Seb shrugged again. 'Not sure, but since I dyed my hair back to brown, Father seems to be satisfied.' Grace smiled. 'Do you want to see a photo? Personally I think it looked awesome.'

With a few quick finger taps, he handed Grace his phone. She felt as if her heart had stopped, but it was not due to the sight of Seb with electric-blue hair. Seb was grinning at the camera with one thumb up, his other arm slung around the other person. That person was Adam.

Grace marvelled that he hadn't changed. He still had the same movie-star good looks, and if anything, seemed to have grown into his features. He was a little taller than she remembered, and broader. His hair was messy, as if he had just run his hand through it, and his sparkling blue eyes showed that his smile was coming from the inside.

Grace realised that she had been staring at Seb's phone for some time. 'Sorry,' she said, dragging her eyes away and wishing in that moment that she hadn't come; that she had come up with an excuse. She could feel Seb's eyes studying her just as his older brother's had done when they were at school.

'I'm sorry, Gracie. I didn't mean to upset you.'

She forced a look of composure onto her face. The three years since she had begun playing with a national orchestra had given her ample opportunity to practise her best 'performance face', designed to hide all manner of fears and nerves. 'You didn't,' she said, trying to put brightness in her voice. 'Your hair was pretty spectacular,' she added, hoping to change the subject.

'He talks about you all the time, you know,' Seb said.

Grace raised a slightly disbelieving eyebrow. 'When your father's not around.' None of it was Seb's fault, but she thought she detected something like blame in his voice. 'We were just kids, Seb, and we cared a lot about each other. But that's all in the past. It's so good to see you, though. What are you doing with yourself these days?'

Seb paused for a moment, but seemed to have got the message that Grace didn't want to talk any more about Adam. 'I'm at college, studying art,' he replied, his grin now so wide he looked as if he would split in half. Grace gave him a delighted smile in return. 'I know, I know. I didn't think Father would let me do anything so frivolous, and I think he was secretly hoping that I would grow out of it and do something sensible.' Grace laughed. 'I caught him at a weak moment when I was really sick, and made him promise me that if I survived I could study what I wanted. He agreed, though whether it was because he thought I was a goner or because he thought he'd be able to persuade me to do something dull and boring like law, I don't know.'

Grace let out a peal of laughter and Seb joined her. 'So where are you studying?' she asked him.

'University of Arts, right here in London.'

Grace frowned as she attempted to do some quick mental arithmetic, which had never been her strongest point. She stopped when she saw Seb's grin.

'I'm seventeen, Gracie. I got early acceptance. One of the very few advantages of being home-schooled is that you can go at the pace you want. I finished my A-levels two years early, and they liked my pieces so . . . ' He shrugged like it was nothing. 'I got in.'

Grace shook her head. 'That's amazing, Seb. Really. It's a great school, and hard to get into, I'm told.'

His nonchalant attitude slipped a little as colour rose in his cheeks. 'Yep. Father is soo proud.' He drew out the syllable, and Grace laughed again. In her memories she had somehow forgotten how funny he was. She took another sip of her coffee, which by now was lukewarm, and paused when she saw the concerned look on Seb's face. There was a blast of chilly air as the door opened and closed.

'Seb! There you are. Sorry, mate, but I'm parked on double yellows, so we need to move it.'

Grace watched as Seb opened his mouth, but no words came out. He swallowed and then seemed to find his voice. 'You said you'd text.'

'I know, kid. I'm sorry, but there's no parking out there, so we need to run. Sorry to deprive you of time with your girl — ' The word 'friend' died on

Adam's lips. Grace had turned around in her seat to see who it was and was as still as a statue, unable to move. She stared, as did Adam, and nobody spoke. Moments passed, and the noise from the busy coffee shop seemed to fade away. To Grace, it felt as if they could have been on a desert island in that moment.

'Grace?' Adam was the first to speak. His voice seemed to come from a time long since gone — one that Grace had boxed up in her head, never to be thought of again.

'Hello,' she managed, feeling as if she should say something more but having no idea what. Adam, her first love, was standing here in front of her in some random coffee shop in London. Then the thought struck her that maybe it wasn't so random, and she turned back to look at Seb.

However, one look at his face told her that this had not been his plan at all. He looked pale, and concern was etched across his face, which made Grace want to reach out and tell him that it was okay. But she had no time, as Seb stood up so abruptly that he knocked his chair down behind him. Some of the people sitting nearby paused in their conversations but, seeing nothing interesting happening, they returned to their lattes.

We have to go,' Seb said in a jumbled hurry. 'The car . . . ' He didn't finish his sentence as, with his head down and not looking at his brother, he ran for the door. Grace and Adam watched him and then returned to their staring. It was almost as if each was re-memorising the other's face, which had not been forgotten but simply changed with time.

'Adam!' Seb's voice was urgent. 'I think I see a traffic warden.'

Adam dragged his eyes away to glance out of the window. 'We have to go,' he said, then frowned at his own obvious statement.

Grace nodded, not knowing what to say.

'It was good to see you, Grace.' And then he was gone.

2

Grace knew she should make more effort to pay attention to her friend's conversation. Katie, an oboe player, and Pria, second violin, were having an animated discussion about what had put their conductor in such an appalling temper. It was not an uncommon discussion, but one which they had fairly regularly due to Maestro Bonevere's ever-changing moods.

'Grace?' She blinked in recognition of her name. 'Honestly, girl,' Pria admonished her, 'you're not listening at all! Your surprise visitor the other night really has got you in a spin!'

After much badgering, Grace had admitted to her friends that she had run into an old boyfriend, but had said little else, despite their best efforts to wheedle some more information from her.

'Your ex must be really quite something,' Katie said. 'I'm sure I saw you nearly come in at the wrong point during the second half. Thank god we have a night off tomorrow! Fancy a drink?'

Pria nodded her assent, but Grace shook her head. 'Not me, thanks. I'm heading for a hot bath.'

'Alone?' Pria asked with a giggle.

Grace rolled her eyes. 'I told you, we just bumped into each other. I don't have his number or anything.'

'If you say so.' Katie laughed. 'We'll be on our mobiles if you change your mind.'

They hugged briefly. Grace watched her friends head off towards the local nightlife hotspot, then turned to head for the Tube and home.

A cough made her pull up short, as did the figure leaning against the railings that ran around the concert hall. Warily, she scanned the streets: a few people were still leaving the hall, but no one was near enough for her to catch up to. The figure walked forward unsteadily, and Grace suspected that he was drunk. She strode quickly past, holding herself up tall; she had lived in London for some time and knew that a display of confidence was important.

'Grace,' the voice rasped; and despite all her instincts which told her not to, she turned round. It took her a moment to recognise Seb. His face had a yellow tinge and was glistening with a fine layer of sweat. He swayed a little, and Grace rushed forward to steady him.

'Seb! You look terrible. What's happened to you?' She couldn't believe the change in him over just a couple of days.

'I needed to tell you I'm sorry,' he said before breaking off with a hacking cough. Grace led him back to the wall and eased him down to sit on it.

'Sorry for what? Seb, I need to get you home.'

He shook his head vigorously.

'You must think I planned it, but I didn't. I just wanted to see you and find out how you were doing. But then

Adam came in — he was supposed to text, not just turn up. And now he's upset too . . . ' He paused to take in a breath, which looked painful.

'Does he know you're here?' Grace asked, even though she knew the answer: there was no way Adam would have let Seb go anywhere in this state.

'Doesn't matter,' Seb replied, anger filling his voice.

'Seb, give me your phone.' It was a command, the kind someone would use on their little brother when they meant business.

Seb looked at Grace for a moment and then handed her his phone. She scrolled through the contacts and found Adam's number, then touched 'dial'. Seb made a half-hearted effort to take the phone off her, which only resulted in him nearly losing his balance. Grace used her free hand to steady him.

The phone was answered on the first ring. 'Seb? Where the hell are you?'

'It's Grace. I have Seb here with me, and he looks bad.'

146

'Grace?' The confusion in Adam's voice was evident, but he quickly switched gears. 'Where are you?' he asked tersely, and for a moment Grace wondered if he was mad at her.

'The Concert Hall in Kensington. We're about halfway to the Tube station.'

'Don't move. Keep Seb with you. I'll be there in five.' And then he hung up. Grace stared at the phone for a moment and then handed it back to Seb, who she realised had been paying close attention to the conversation despite everything.

'He's pretty mad,' he commented.

'D'ya think?' Grace said, and then put her arm around his shoulders and pulled him into a one-armed hug.

The next hour passed in a blur. Grace helped Adam lift Seb into his car, and then without being asked climbed in beside him so that Adam could concentrate on driving. The latter said nothing, but Grace was sure she could see gratefulness in his eyes.

'We're nearly there, buddy,' Adam said with forced brightness. 'Just hang on.' Grace caught his gaze in the rear-view mirror and nodded in what she hoped was a confident manner. All the fight seemed to have gone out of Seb, who was leaning against her with his eyes closed as if keeping them open was more than he could manage. Grace squeezed his hand and prayed that everything would be all right.

'Chillax, mother hen,' he said. 'I'm fine. It's just a cold.'

Grace could see Adam's shoulders tense. 'You know you need to be careful, Seb,' he scolded his brother. 'What were you thinking? I leave you alone for twelve hours, and find you miles away from home looking like death. Why didn't you call me?'

'I needed to see Grace. It was important.'

'More important than your health, Seb? I thought we'd got through all that.'

Grace wanted to ask what was going

on but knew that now was not the right time. Adam's car swerved around a taxi and then cut across a line of traffic into a side road. Two minutes later they were pulling into an ambulance bay. A security guard stepped forward, but when he saw Adam, his comment died on his lips.

'Get me a trolley,' Adam said to him, running to the back door of the car. He pulled it open and, with help from Grace, managed to get Seb out of the car. The trolley arrived, as did a nurse whom Adam seemed to know. Between them they lifted Seb on to the trolley. Seb had hold of Grace's hand and didn't seem willing to let go, so she hurried beside them as they made their way into the emergency department.

'Miss, you need to step outside,' a petite nurse with shiny brown hair said. Grace nodded, but Seb wouldn't let go of her hand and tried to sit up on the trolley. Adam pushed him gently back.

'She's with me,' said Adam, glancing up at Grace, his face somehow a mess of both fear and professionalism. Then he turned back to focus on his brother. Someone brought Grace a stool to sit on, and she watched all the purposeful activity around her, wishing she could do something more useful. All she could do was hold Seb's hand and hope, so she did.

★ ★ ★

She stayed with Seb, even when he had a chest x-ray. Adam had tried to persuade Seb to let her go outside, but he got so agitated that Grace looked at Adam and he wordlessly handed her a heavy apron so that she could stay by his side. Seb was transferred to the high dependency unit and wired up to all manner of machines. His breathing seemed easier with the oxygen mask, and before long he fell asleep.

'I need to call my father,' Adam said to Grace. 'Do you mind staying? I know it's late, but I'd rather he wasn't alone.' He ran his hand through his hair and

Grace felt like she was sixteen again.

'Of course. Take all the time you need.'

He looked as if he wanted to say something more, but decided better of it, and left the room. Grace wondered if he would ever find his voice; if they would ever be able to have a conversation. She wasn't sure that she wanted to talk to him about the past — it had taken her years to move on; but now that he was here in front of her, she knew that old feelings were stirring within her, and that soon she would have a decision to make. It was like standing on a cliff, deciding whether or not to jump. If she let those feelings out of the box she had forced them into, she was not sure how long it would take her to put them back.

Lost in thought, she didn't realise that Adam had come back into the room. A paper cup of coffee was wafted in front of her eyes. 'Here, I thought you might need a drink.'

'Thanks,' she said, looking up. His

face was creased with worry still, and she knew that Seb was not out of the woods. 'How did it go with your father?'

'About the same as usual: I should never have let Seb move in with me; I had no idea what it takes to look after him. Same old, same old.'

'I'm sorry,' Grace said, reaching out and squeezing his hand.

'Don't be. It's taken a while, but I've accepted that I'll never be the man my father wants me to be.'

A beat passed between them.

'He's wrong, you know,' Grace said eventually. 'Seb worships you; he always has. I've never seen a person take better care of his brother.'

'Maybe you could tell my father that,' Adam said managing a rueful smile.

'Now we both know that would *not* be a good plan.' Grace took a sip of the hot, bitter machine-dispensed coffee, which tasted surprisingly good.

'He was never exactly my biggest fan.'

'Yeah well, he's a jerk who wouldn't know a decent person if they came up and bit him on the butt — which, considering they were a decent person, would probably never happen.' She laughed despite the situation and was relieved when Adam joined her.

'Do you two mind?' came Seb's amused, albeit weak, voice. 'Some of us sick people are trying to get some sleep here.'

Adam stood up and moved so that he could check the monitors. Seemingly satisfied, he said, 'You told me it was just a cold.'

'I may have understated things a little.' Seb coughed and Adam put a hand on his shoulder.

'Easy, buddy.'

Seb opened his eyes, clearly with some effort. 'Would you two get out of here? Seriously, it's hard to sleep with all that pent-up romantic energy flying between you.' The effort seemed too much, and he closed his eyes.

Adam seemed to be studiously

avoiding catching Grace's eye. 'I'll ask one of the nurses to get you a cab.'

Seb's voice drifted from the bed: 'Good. You can share one.'

'I'm not going anywhere,' Adam said firmly.

'No offence, bro, but I'm not a kid. All I'm planning to do is sleep, and you staring at me all night is surprisingly not that relaxing.' When Adam didn't move, Seb said: 'We live five minutes away. They'll call if I need you.'

Adam leaned in and looked his brother in the eye. 'If you're sure.'

'Go!' Seb said, and Adam kissed him on the head.

'Behave. I'll be back at six.'

'Make it eight. I think I'm in need of a lie-in.' Seb managed a weak smile and then turned his head away, unable to fight sleep any longer.

'Good night, Seb,' Grace said softly.

'Night, Gracie,' Seb whispered, half-asleep.

3

Grace and Adam walked down the dimly lit hospital corridors in silence. The building at night seemed to take on the persona of a church sanctuary, quiet and solemn. Despite the fact that it was now well past midnight, Grace's mind flitted between concern for Seb and the mixed-up emotions she was feeling about seeing Adam after all these years. She risked a glance and saw that his face was composed, almost shut down, so there was no way to know what he was thinking. The only sound was the noise of her shoes on the lino floor.

'I can get a cab,' she said, feeling the need suddenly to do something with the silence.

Adam looked at her as if he had suddenly remembered she was there. It gave Grace a stab of pain, which she quickly brushed away as being selfish and unreasonable under the current circumstances. But despite her best efforts, the dull ache that she lived with every day seemed to grow in strength.

'I mean, you have your car, and you need to be close to the hospital,' she added. 'I live miles away, so it makes sense . . . ' Her voice trailed off.

'Actually, I was wondering if you would stay the night,' Adam said.

Grace stopped walking. Despite her best efforts, she felt an eyebrow raise, and her arms seemed to cross themselves. All of a sudden she felt sixteen again. She stayed where she was, and counted out Adam's steps. He walked seven steps before he realised that she was no longer by his side.

'Are you okay?' he asked, frowning.

'I'm not sure what to say to that,' Grace replied. As Adam continued to look confused, she reminded him: 'You asked me to stay the night.'

He nodded. 'If you don't mind. I don't fancy being in the flat on my own.'

Grace watched as realisation dawned,

and she made a half-hearted effort not to smile.

'Ah . . . that's not what I meant, obviously. I don't want you to think that . . .'

Grace laughed then. She couldn't be absolutely sure, as the lighting was so dim, but it really did look like Adam was blushing. She savoured the moment, feeling the closeness that they had once shared, then walked towards him and slid an arm through his.

'Relax, Adam. I knew what you meant.' With her other hand, she crossed her fingers to ward off the little white lie she was telling. 'It's late — actually, I think it is probably classed as early — and I don't have a concert tonight, so yes, I'll keep you company.'

He looked relieved, and there was a sparkle in his eyes that had been missing with all the worry. 'The bad news is that I still can't cook,' he told her ruefully. She nodded. 'The good news is that I live over a twenty-four-hour diner, so you can get cheeseburgers at — ' He

lifted his wrist to look at his watch.
' — three thirty in the morning.'

★ ★ ★

Adam's flat, Grace decided, looked as if a hard-working doctor and his teenage younger brother lived there. It was kitted out with all the latest technology in terms of music, TV and gaming, but was distinctly lacking in the kitchen department. Grace had opened every cupboard and had yet to find a glass to pour her drink into.

'Sorry,' Adam said when he noticed her searching. 'We pretty much broke them all; and since we tend to drink straight out of a can or bottle, we haven't bothered to replace them.' He grinned up at her from the long sofa that sat across one wall. The kitchen range sat along the opposite. The flat was much larger than her tiny attic flat but, she decided, lacked a certain charm.

'You let Seb drink beer?'

'On occasion. As he keeps telling me,

he's not a kid anymore.'

Grace sat opposite Adam in a lounging chair and picked up her cheeseburger. When Adam had said they were the best in London, she had been unconvinced, and when she had seen the diner she had been even more so. But the burger was delicious, and she was surprised at how hungry she was despite the fact it was now four a.m.

'Enjoying that?' Adam asked as Grace tried to delicately wipe away the splodge of ketchup that was running down her chin.

'You were right,' she said with a shrug.

'Told you.'

She watched as he checked his mobile and pager. Finally she asked: 'So, what's going on with Seb?'

Adam leaned back into the sofa and took a swig of cola. 'Where do you want me to start? He had a lung transplant two years ago. Physically he's done really, well but emotionally not so much.'

'Must be tough thinking that you're only alive and feeling better because someone else isn't.'

Adam leaned forward. 'Did he tell you that, or are you just as perceptive as ever?'

Grace shrugged. 'He told me a little.'

'He's been to counselling, which I think helped. But now he seems to be on a mission to right some wrongs.'

Grace raised an eyebrow, but waited for Adam to speak again.

'He keeps trying to fix my relationship with our father, like he thinks somehow we don't get on because of something he did, or because he was sick . . . And then there's you.' He stopped and looked at Grace, and she surprised herself when she found she could hold his gaze.

'So coming to find me was not because he has an enduring love of classical music played by a full orchestra?'

'He's more of a jazz fan,' Adam said. A moment of silence seemed to roll out between them, and neither wanted to be the first to speak. Then Adam's phone beeped and he picked it up.

Grace could see carefully guarded fear in his eyes, but his tense shoulders relaxed a little.

'Just Mum,' he explained when he had ended the call. 'They're on their way back from France and should be at the hospital by eleven.' Grace said nothing as Adam texted back a quick reply. 'Well that'll be a fun reunion,' he said, seemingly to himself.

'It's not your fault that Seb's poorly.'

'Father won't see it that way. Seb's on some pretty heavy-duty anti-rejection drugs. They suppress your immune system, which is good for your new organs, but no so good for fighting off infections.'

'So a normal cold for you or me would be something serious for Seb?'

'It could turn into a nasty chest infection, yes. His bloods weren't too bad and his chest x-ray was OK, so barring any complications he should be fine.'

'Hard not to worry, though.'

Adam nodded, looking as if he had the weight of the world on his shoulders.

'When do you have to be back at work?' Grace asked him.

'Tomorrow afternoon. A mate's covering for me.' Adam yawned and rubbed a hand across his face.

'Maybe you should get some sleep. I can get a cab, or stay and keep an eye on your mobile if you're worried you won't hear it.'

Grace tried to pin down her feelings. More than anything, if she were honest, she wanted to stay; but since she had been unable to read Adam's feelings, it was probably not a good plan.

'Why don't you get some sleep here?' he suggested. 'Then we could go and visit Seb together.'

Adam's voice sounded hopeful, and Grace was about to agree, when she remembered that his parents would be arriving. The look on her face must have given away her thoughts.

'I'll set the alarm so we can get there before them,' he said. 'You can have my bed or Seb's, or the sofa's quite comfy.' The last sentence came out in a rush and Grace couldn't help smiling again.

'You go to bed,' she said. 'You need to get some sleep before work. I'll crash on the sofa and listen out for the phone.'

Grace hugged herself as she waited for Adam to go and find her a blanket and pillow. She knew that she might be reading more into his desire for her to stay than was actually there, but it was a thrilling feeling nonetheless. Years might have gone by; but despite her best efforts, her feelings for him remained, and nothing she had seen of him in the last ten hours had changed her mind at all. She took the blanket and pillow from his outstretched hand and realised that he was looking at her closely.

'Thanks for this,' he said quietly. 'For staying with me. I don't deserve you.'

Grace blinked and wondered what he meant. His face said he wanted to say more, but he seemed to shake it off, and then stepped away and closed the door behind him.

4

Grace heard the door click closed and wondered for a moment who was in her flat. As her eyes adjusted to the sudden brightness, the memories of the previous night returned. Glancing at her watch, she wondered if she had overslept, thinking that Adam had gone to visit Seb without her. Her watch said eight-thirty. Picking up Adam's phone, she saw that there were no new messages or missed calls.

The door opened, and Adam stepped in with two paper cups and a bag which had all the outward signs and promise of something made of pastry and full of calories. 'Morning again,' he said. 'I thought we might need a pick-me-up before we visited Seb. The food at the hospital is lousy, so I got some for him too.' He handed her a coffee, which she took a grateful sip of. Then she took a

164

bite from an almond croissant, dropping flakes into her lap. The croissant was delicious, and she looked up at Adam with a querying eye.

'Next to the best diner in London is the best French patisserie. Seb and I checked out the food before we moved in.'

Grace, with her mouth full, could only nod in appreciation. She took a moment to swallow and then realised that if she didn't ask soon, she never would. 'What did you mean last night, about not deserving me?' She hoped she knew the answer, and watched Adam closely as he moved to sit on the coffee table, so close now that she could reach out for him. He took a sip of coffee, appearing to compose his thoughts, and then looked at her.

'I meant,' he said carefully, 'that I was not a good friend to you when we were at school. You, on the other hand, have always been good to me — which you demonstrated again last night. And, well, I wanted to let you know that I appreciate it.' He frowned now, as if his own words weren't exactly making sense to him.

For all the intervening years, Grace had wondered what she would say to Adam if she saw him again. For a good few of those years, when the pain was less raw, all she felt was anger and hurt and the desire to explain to him exactly what he had done to her. But now, faced with him in front of her, she had the overwhelming desire to erase some of his guilt.

'It was a long time ago, Adam, and we were just kids.'

'Yeah, I tried convincing myself of that. But the truth is, I should have stuck up for you. I should have gone to the headmaster and told him that you weren't the person Arabella had made you out to be. I should have exposed her and every other phony thing about the school, but I didn't.' He shrugged helplessly, as if he wanted to go back and change things right at that moment. Grace considered his words, knowing deep down that those events were not the ones that had hurt her the most.

'He wouldn't have believed you, Adam, and the outcome would've been the same.'

'Would it?'

Grace was surprised now. 'I would still have been expelled. I would still have left the school.'

'But if I hadn't let you down when you needed me, then maybe you would've tried to keep in touch.'

Grace felt her grip on her paper coffee cup loosen a little, and she had to move her other hand to steady it. She wanted to look at Adam but was afraid of what her expression might give away. Her mind raced as she remembered all the letters that she had written to him, and all the times she had begged him to write back, even if it was to tell her it was over. Somehow the pain of rejection would have been less than the pain of being ignored and forgotten. She had written every day at first; it was the only thing that kept her going as she had to readjust to her old life, as well as coping with her parents' concern for her and their anger at the school that had expelled her for what they had been sure was a lie. But slowly she had been forced to accept the truth in front of her: Adam either didn't care about her anymore, or maybe never had. And so she had stopped sending him the letters that she wrote.

'I'm going to get my things together,' Adam said. 'We need to get a move on if you want to avoid my parents.'

His voice was dull, and Grace knew that he had expected more from her. Her silence had probably been interpreted as embarrassment at not knowing what to say about her lack of contact. What she did not understand was why he had not received her letters. She had posted them herself. She knew she had the right address, as she and Adam had swapped; it was one of the last things they had done before her fateful meeting with the school board. All thoughts of the mystery were suddenly banished by the most obvious question: why had *he* not written to *her*? The guilt she felt at letting him, even for a moment, believe that she had not bothered to try and stay in touch was quickly replaced by a flash of anger that was all too familiar.

She looked up as Adam walked back in to the room, shrugging on his coat, with keys in his hand. 'Why didn't you?' she asked. In her head she was continuing with their last conversation. Adam appeared momentarily confused, but the look was quickly replaced by something else.

'We need to go,' he said.

Grace knew he was trying to change the subject, and stood her ground. 'I think you need to answer my question.' Inwardly she cringed at the tone she knew she was taking.

'Why? You didn't answer mine.'

Grace raised an eyebrow. 'What? Are we still teenagers?'

'Apparently. Are you coming?' Adam had walked away from her to the door. She didn't want to leave; she wanted them to talk about what had happened, preferably like adults. But one glance at the clock told her that if she wanted to see Seb, they did indeed need to go now.

'Can we meet later, so we can talk? Talk properly, I mean,' Grace said, forcing herself to remember that she was a mature adult now and could behave like one.

'I have to work,' Adam replied before opening the front door. 'But I should finish around five tomorrow. Maybe we could meet for coffee?'

He did not look happy about the idea, and Grace wondered again if she were ready to open the box of emotions that she had so carefully packed away in her mind. A conversation with Adam, even as an adult, might well fill in some of the blank spaces in their story; but the truth of those gaps had great power to hurt her, even now after all these years. The doubt was gone: for a long time she had wondered what she would do if this moment ever arose; and now she knew. She wanted — no, *needed*

— to know the whole story, however painful it might be. Only then could she truly close that chapter of her life and move on.

★ ★ ★

Seb was sitting up in bed and, although wired up to a heart monitor and various bags of fluid and antibiotics, was a healthier colour than the previous evening. Grace handed over the paper bag with pastry goodies whilst Adam checked in with the nursing staff.

'You are an absolute life-saver,' Seb said to his brother through a mouthful of cream doughnut. 'I'm starving!'

Grace pulled up a chair and sat down, feeling relief wash over her. She could not completely rid herself of the nagging doubt that she had somehow contributed to Seb being so unwell. If she had said something different the night they had met, then maybe he wouldn't have risked everything to come and find her again.

'I take that as a good sign,' she said, then glanced at her watch.

'Their flight gets in soon, but it'll take them a while to cross London,' Seb said.

Grace nodded. 'That obvious huh?'

Seb smiled thinly. 'I don't blame you for not wanting to see my father, not after what he did.' He bit down on the chocolate éclair that he had also found in the bag.

'You mean the letters?' Grace said the words just as her brain had made the connection, and she watched Seb closely for his reaction. He stopped eating and swallowed like it was quite an effort, then glanced over Grace's shoulder, and she knew he was checking where Adam was.

'How did you find out?' he asked her.

'You just told me,' Grace said with a wry smile. 'Adam asked me last night why I'd never been in touch, and I couldn't figure out why he hadn't received my letters. I posted them myself, so I know the problem wasn't at my end. It's the only logical explanation, which you just confirmed by the look on your face.'

'Adam doesn't know,' Seb said, leaning forward before he started to cough. It seemed to ripple through his body and was clearly painful.

'Seb, it's okay, ssh, it's okay. I haven't said anything to Adam about what I suspected.' Grace was standing beside Seb, holding on to the hand nearest to her and using her other to brush his hair away from his forehead.

'Adam would never forgive him,' Seb wheezed.

Grace nodded. 'I know, and I don't want to get between them. I didn't back then, and I don't now. Family is too important.'

Seb seemed to relax a little, and Grace lifted the oxygen mask that was dangling around his neck, gently placing it over his mouth. 'Take it easy, will you? I'll get thrown out for upsetting a patient.' She pulled her chair forward and sat down. Seb's tight grip told her that he wasn't ready for her to leave just yet. 'I won't tell him, Seb, I promise.' The words were painful to say, but it was a personal pain, and she knew after years of practice that she could bear it. What she couldn't bear was seeing Seb so distressed; and she knew that if she told Adam, she risked tearing their family apart, which would only bring more pain all round. In that moment Grace knew she could not do that to Seb or Adam. She cared about — no, loved — them too much.

Grace knew what she had to do. Firstly, she needed to get out before Adam's father arrived. She could cope with everything else; but whether she could hold her emotions in if she was confronted with him face to face, she wasn't so sure.

'I have to go, Seb. Your folks will be here soon.' He shook his head. 'I need to take a shower and put on some clean clothes; feed the cat — you know, all the mundane stuff. But I'll keep in touch and come and see you in a few days.'

Seb's eyes studied her closely, as if he were checking to see if she were telling the truth.

'I promise. Here, give me your phone. I'll put my number in it, and then you can text me if I don't come and see you.' This seemed to pacify him, and he handed her his phone. Grace stood, quickly entered her number, and then gave the phone back to Seb for his approval. He nodded, and she leaned over and kissed him on the forehead.

'See you soon, Gracie,' he whispered.

'You bet, kid.' Grace smiled and then headed for the door, which opened just as her hand reached out. She stiffened, worried that Seb's parents were early, but Adam stood before her.

'Leaving?' he asked.

Grace nodded. 'Stuff to do. And you all need to be together as a family.'

'You're probably right. We still on for coffee?'

'Yes, if you want to. I gave Seb my number. Give me a call.'

And with that, Grace walked quickly away, wondering if Adam would call and if she really wanted him to.

5

Grace stood at the entry to the Tube station, lost in a sea of indecision. If she didn't want to be horribly late, then she needed to move, but her feet just wouldn't obey. Her promise to Seb was all she could think about. If she told Adam that she had written to him, he would want to know why he had never received her letters; she had figured it out quickly herself, and knew it would only take him a matter of moments. It would therefore be necessary to lie, or at least tell a half-truth — which didn't sit well with her; but she also knew what was at stake. She could not break her promise to Seb, with all the potential consequences of that, so she had to either stand Adam up or find a way to explain the lack of letters.

After a few more deep, steadying breaths, Grace made up her mind, then stepped out of the station and headed towards the café. She saw Adam before he saw her. He was sitting in an armchair by the window. A newspaper lay on the table in front of him, which he ignored, and a cup of coffee sat next to it, untouched. Grace pushed open the door and was hit by a wave of heat and the strong smell of freshly ground coffee beans. Adam looked up and smiled, somehow managing to express a mixture of self-confidence and well-hidden fear. Grace smiled to herself: it was good to know she wasn't the only one who was a little nervous about the conversation they were going to have.

She sat in the seat opposite Adam and concentrated on removing her scarf and gloves as well as her coat, to give herself a few precious extra seconds to compose herself.

'Tea, coffee?' Adam offered. 'I'd personally recommend the hot chocolate due to the generous application of marshmallows.'

'Since all of your food recommendations have been spot on so far, I guess a hot chocolate would be good.'

Adam grinned and caught the eye of the waitress, who seemed to know him. With a nod, he seemed to communicate his order.

'You come here a lot then?' Grace asked him, settling on a safe topic.

'Used to pull all-nighters studying here. While I crammed, they kept me well supplied with brain food.'

Grace raised an eyebrow. She couldn't see any fish or any other food that might be deemed good for the brain.

'You know,' Adam said, interpreting her glance, 'hot chocolate, muffins, pastries and extra-shot espresso. What more could a medical student need?' He opened his arms in an expansive gesture and Grace laughed.

'You seemed to have had a different student experience to me. Mine was more value-brands and eating a lot of toast.'

He studied her for a moment, and she felt the gap in their wealth stand between them again as it had at school. 'I know I'm one of the lucky ones.' He seemed to be apologising.

'I didn't mean it quite like that. I hope you know me better than that.' Her words spilt out as they always did when she felt she had said the wrong thing.

'I do,' he said, and smiled. 'Anyway, it's good to be reminded. Sometimes I forget I've had it easy, especially after a few days of dealing with my father.'

Grace grimaced in sympathy. 'That bad?'

Adam shrugged. 'About the same as usual. Seb's doing better, though. He'll need to stay in for a few more days, but then he should be okay to be discharged.'

Grace saw something flash across his face. 'Discharged back to yours?' she asked, taking a spoon to the marshmallows on her hot chocolate that had just arrived invitingly in front of her.

'My father thinks I am not a fit guardian; that I don't take care of Seb. In essence, that I'm not up to scratch in all areas of my life, professional and personal.'

'Ah, that bad. And what does Seb have to say about it?'

'Seb's working on our father, but I think he'll have to admit defeat and go and stay with them for a couple of weeks at least.'

'I'm sorry,' Grace said, and she meant it. Since she had met Adam, she knew that she would not have swapped her relationship with her parents for the wealth that Adam had and the luxurious lifestyle it offered.

'As I said before, don't be. That ship has long sailed, and it's taken a while, but I can genuinely say that my father's opinion means very little to me anymore.'

Grace leaned forward and rested her chin in her hands. 'Family is important, though, Adam.'

He snorted a laugh. 'Family like yours is important. Family like mine, or at least a father like mine, is not. I can't live up to his expectations; I've never been able to. So now I just make life easy by accepting that I never will.'

Grace said nothing; just smiled reassuringly. It was clear that Adam needed to have a good vent.

'If it wasn't for Seb, I wouldn't bother,' he continued. 'Of course, Father would probably cut me off. But I earn a living now — not that junior doctors are well paid, but I could get by.' He turned to stare out of the window again; but then, remembering where he was and who he was with, he added, 'Anyway, enough of my car-crash relationship with my father. How are your folks?'

'Good.' Grace smiled. 'Dad only has another few years and then he'll retire. Mum has a few more after that, and then they plan to take their campervan wherever they want to go.'

'Sounds like a great plan. I'd love to do something like that — just take off with no purpose other than exploring. Doing what you want when you want.'

'Anything's possible,' Grace said.

'What's stopping you? As a doctor, you could travel where you want; work where you want. You could do charity work or paid work.'

'I wonder what my father would have to say about that. It would probably be the cherry on the cake of disappointment.'

Grace had taken a sip of hot chocolate at just the wrong moment and spent several minutes coughing and giggling until tears rolled down her cheeks.

'I missed you, Gracie,' Adam said. 'You are the most real person I know, except for Seb.'

Grace swallowed as her mouth seemed to dry up. She had spent many years wondering if Adam would ever say those words to her again. 'I missed you, too,' she said, watching as him slowly moved his hand across the table between them to squeeze her hand.

'When I didn't hear from you,' he said, 'I guess I convinced myself that you wanted me to stay away, so I stopped fighting Father about it. He thought he had won; that I had finally listened to him, and I got to see Seb.'

Grace could hear the reproach in his voice and knew she needed to say something. She tried to run through the options she had come up with in the intervening days; the things she could say that might be close enough to the truth but not cause Adam more pain, or end up being the straw that broke the camel's back where his father was concerned.

'It was difficult . . . ' she began, and then took a sip of her now-lukewarm hot chocolate. 'I was so upset, and Mum and Dad were distraught. I had to get into my local college and try and rebuild my life.' She fiddled with her scarf in her lap, hoping that Adam would say something; but when he didn't, she was forced to look up. He was listening to her closely, and there were both pain and understanding in his expression.

'I never meant to hurt you,' Grace said, knowing her voice was pleading. 'Really, I didn't, Adam. But I was worried that if we kept in touch, it would just cause us more pain . . . ' Her voice faded away as the lies died on her tongue.

Adam thought for a moment, then sighed. 'We were just kids and we both made mistakes. For my part, I should never have let my father bully me. And you . . . maybe you should have trusted me more.' He threw his hands in the air like he wasn't sure what to say.

Grace wanted to say that she did trust him, *had* trusted him, but she knew she couldn't. 'So what now?' she asked, not knowing what else to say.

Adam leaned forward again, and she felt captured in his gaze. 'For the first time,' he answered, 'I guess that's entirely up to us.'

6

Grace checked her appearance in the mirror one more time. The tannoy had announced that the curtain would go up in ten minutes, and she needed to get onstage. She smoothed down her crushed-velvet black dress and lifted a hand to check that her hair was still held in a loose chignon by numerous pins. She was distracted by the sounds of giggling from behind her and looked in the mirror more closely to see Katie and Pria goggling at her.

'Anyone would think someone important was coming to watch you play tonight!' Pria said loudly, and a few of their fellow musicians turned around. Grace rolled her eyes at her friends in the mirror.

'I'm not sure who's more excited, you or me!' Katie said, stepping up behind her and pulling her into a quick hug. 'I can't believe that we finally get to meet him!'

Grace couldn't help but grin, remembering the day at the café when she and Adam had decided that they wanted to get to know each other again and see where it went. They had started with meeting for coffee, but they had quickly become more than friends. In many respects it was like they had never been apart; and now he was coming to see her play, having finally got an evening off when her orchestra was in London. Grace felt like she was about to step back into 'her' practice room at Henry Tyndale, knowing that Adam would be waiting there to hear her play.

The bell sounded and Grace followed Pria, Katie and the other members of the orchestra she shared a dressing room with, down to the stairs that led up to the central stage. She could imagine that Adam was there, maybe scanning the programme for her name, looking around and waiting for them to play; waiting for her. She knew when the curtains went up that she wouldn't be able to see beyond the front row due to the bright lights, but she felt sure she would know that he was there. She closed her eyes, and in that moment she was back in the practice room, just her and Adam. The tap of the baton on the music stand brought her back to the present, and she lifted her violin to her chin, ready to play.

★ ★ ★

The orchestra stood as one and bowed again, the sound of clapping swirling around the high domed hall. Grace could not help but smile as they bowed one final time before leaving the stage. She followed the other musicians and had just reached the wings when a voice called her up short.

'Mizz Taylor?' The accent was unmistakably French, which meant only one thing: it was the conductor, Monsieur Bonevere. Grace felt her heart speed up just a little. She was so sure that the concert had gone well; she thought that she had played her part too.

'Yes, monsieur?' she said, forcing her voice to be steady and calm.

'You 'ave played well this evening. Monsieur Bonevere is very pleased.'

Grace blinked. Having prepared herself for what inevitably would be some kind of telling-off, she could not quite believe her ears. Monsieur Bonevere had never spoken to her unless it was to give her stern advice about her playing and what she needed to improve on. In fact, she had never heard him praise anyone before, not even the soloists.

'Thank you, monsieur,' she managed to say before he swept through the wings, clicking his fingers at one of his assistants. She was rooted to the spot, not sure what to make of what had just happened.

'Adam must be quite a guy,' Pria said. Grace jumped, not having realised that her friend had come up beside her. 'I've never heard any kind of praise come from that man's lips, ever.'

Grace was still trying to understand what had just happened when Katie appeared from behind the curtain. 'There you are!' she said. 'Are you coming or what? I'm desperate to meet your mystery man.' She held her hand out to Grace, who took it and let herself be pulled from the stage.

Grace pushed the side door open. Pria always called it the tradesman's entrance, but really it was to allow the performers to avoid the crush at the main entrance after the performance. She did not have to look far to spot Adam. He was dressed in a very smart, well-cut dark navy suit and tie. He seemed to ooze charm and sophistication. Grace had an overwhelming urge to pinch herself. Only in her wildest dreams had she been able to imagine a future where Adam stepped back into her life and swept her off her feet.

'You're blocking my view,' Pria said impatiently. 'I can't wait another second to meet the famous Adam!'

With Pria nudging her in the back, Grace took a step forward, hoping that the dim lighting might hide her blush. Adam turned at the sound of his name and Grace watched his face break into a broad grin. Naturally he had heard Pria's comment.

'Gracie, you were marvellous,' he told her, then leaned in and kissed her lightly on each cheek in an exaggerated manner. Grace punched him on the arm. Pria and Katie giggled, clearly won over by his charm.

'Pria, Katie, this is Adam,' Grace said. 'Adam, this is Pria and Katie.'

Adam held out his hand and solemnly shook with each of them.

'So, the famous Adam,' Pria said, her eyes glittering with mischief.

'I see my reputation precedes me.' Adam laughed and slung an arm around Grace's shoulders, pulling her in close. Grace rolled her eyes but couldn't help smiling.

'Actually, Grace has been fairly tight-lipped about you,' Katie said with an innocent expression, ignoring Grace's glare.

'I'm an open book,' Adam said, squeezing Grace slightly. 'What do you want to know?'

'Everything,' Pria said. 'Every little detail.'

'Well if you want to know *everything*, we should go get a drink and maybe something to eat. It might take a while.' He released Grace for a moment so that he could grab her hand, and pulled her in the direction of a local bar that had become a bit of a favourite for their 'date nights'.

'Relax — I've got this,' he whispered in Grace's ear. But Grace couldn't relax, despite his reassurance. The last few weeks had been wonderful, there was no doubt about that. The teenage Adam had grown into the man that Grace had always pictured in her mind. He was still funny and goofy, and always ready to tease; but there was a strength to him now, like he was finally happy in his own skin. The face that he presented to the world was the real Adam, and the world could take it or leave it. That part of him had changed. She loved spending time with him, as she always had. She also knew that the love she felt for him had not died or been corrupted by the pain of their separation. She loved him still, and was beginning to allow herself to hope that he loved her too.

But what future could they have with the giant elephant in the room? They had carefully managed to avoid any reference to their parting or the events that had followed, sticking to safer topics about their lives now and what they wanted from their futures. Perhaps they had been too careful. This could not go on. If they wanted a future together, they would need to rip the plaster off of the wound that they both carried. Grace was not sure that it would be best done with the audience of her two close friends, who would undoubtedly ask how they had met and why they had parted. What would Adam say?

'So that's us,' Adam said in conclusion

to the story he had been relating to Pria and Katie. 'Met at school, drifted apart, and then bumped into each other again.'

'It's like an old-fashioned romantic movie,' Katie said in a dreamy voice as she rested her head on her hand and stared at both Adam and Grace.

Grace felt Adam's hand on her knee and she knew he had told what could only be described as the 'edited' version. She took a sip of her drink to give herself a moment to take in her friends' reactions. Katie, ever the romantic, had bought every word, but Pria looked less convinced.

'You never told us that you went to Henry Tyndale,' Pria said to Grace, 'even after all the ghastly stories I told you about my time boarding.'

Grace managed to shrug. 'I was only there a term, then decided it wasn't for me. I missed home too much, and everyone there was so different from what I was used to.' She felt the lie come out so easily that for a moment it felt like the truth.

'But you met Adam,' Katie said with a sigh. 'Wasn't that enough to make you want to stay?'

Grace tried to smile. Katie was desperate to meet her own Prince Charming and had so far been gravely disappointed in the men she had dated, but her words still hurt. Grace knew it wasn't Katie's fault. She hadn't told her the real story, and she knew that if she did Katie would completely understand and be sympathetic.

'Alas, young love is not enough to overcome the bitchiness of fake girls with rich daddies,' Adam said, saving Grace from having to think of something to say.

Pria laughed. 'Yep, it's an unrecognised superpower.' And then thankfully the conversation moved on.

After Katie and Priya had said their goodbyes, Grace and Adam walked down the near-empty street hand in hand. They both had a precious day off tomorrow, so were in no hurry to end their evening.

'That went well,' Adam said, although

it sounded more like a question to Grace.

'Thanks to you,' Grace said, giving his hand a squeeze.

'I wasn't about to tell them everything, Gracie, once it was clear you hadn't told them yourself.'

Grace looked up at him then, wondering if he was cross or hurt, but his face only registered concern. 'It's our story, and well . . . ' She struggled to find the words. Did she really want to start this conversation now? 'We haven't really talked about it, and I'm not sure how you feel about it or what you think . . . ' She let her voice trail off, knowing she had a habit of rambling and saying things without thinking them through first.

'No, we haven't. I kind of got the impression that you didn't want to. Talk about it, I mean.'

Grace smiled. 'That's funny; I got the same impression from you.'

Adam let out a short burst of laughter. 'I just didn't want to ruin things. Everything seemed so perfect, like magic, and I didn't want to burst the bubble.'

'But you know we need to. If we don't, the issue will always be, there and it might break us later.' She added the last bit softly, as if even saying the words aloud might make it happen.

Adam stopped, and Grace didn't realise until she felt a pull on her hand. In one swift movement she was in Adam's arms, and he was kissing her with an urgency that reminded her so much of their last night together that she almost felt she was reliving it.

'We won't let it, Gracie. We won't let it destroy us. I've never been this happy — not since we were last together, and this time I won't let you go whatever happens. I want you in my life. We aren't kids anymore; we can make our own decisions.'

'But you know we need to talk about it?'

Adam nodded but said nothing, as if he knew she had more to say and needed the space to say it.

'I know I hurt you,' she whispered as he leaned in and kissed her gently on the forehead.

'We were children, Gracie. Just kids, and there were influences on us and our decisions then that we couldn't control. That's not true now.'

Grace smiled, although inside she knew she could not completely accept the situation. She gently pulled Adam's face towards her and kissed him.

'I love you, Grace — right now, in this moment. And that's all that really matters.'

'I love you, too,' Grace replied with a smile. She wanted to believe what he'd said — that it was the past and it didn't matter. She wanted to believe he could forgive her for the hurt of not being in contact, but she had seen the pain on his face the first day they had been reunited, and a small part of her doubted it could all be washed away so easily.

7

Grace moved around the kitchen as quietly as she could. She was cooking a roast dinner for Seb and Adam. Adam had arrived home from a busy night shift at nine and had gone to bed for a few hours. Seb was sitting out on the small balcony of the flat he shared with Adam, sketching. 'I'm starving,' he said as he got up and joined Grace in the kitchen.

'It will be about another half-hour, I'm afraid. But fortunately for you, I brought crisps.'

'Gracie, you're the best!' Seb said before stuffing his mouth full.

'No, I just know you have quite the appetite. Have you taken your meds today?'

'Yes, Mum,' Seb said, rolling his eyes and doing a great impression of a stroppy teenager.

'You know you'd forget if we didn't remind you.'

'I'm seventeen, Grace. I can look after myself.'

'Uh huh,' Grace said, but smiled at him. Seb was very much like the little brother she had never had but always wanted. Having Seb in her life was yet another positive thing about being with Adam. 'How's the drawing?' she asked him.

Seb shrugged and Grace knew that sign.

'That good?'

He let out a long sigh. 'Just feels a bit pointless, you know?'

Grace frowned. Seb seemed stuck somehow. He would rally for a few weeks, but then it was like a dark cloud settled over his life and he lost all sense of enjoyment. 'Well, I've been giving that some thought,' she said, wondering if now was a good time to tell Seb about her idea.

'That everything is pointless?'

Grace looked up and noted the small

smile. Seb wasn't quite at his lowest yet. 'I was thinking maybe you need a change.'

He sat down on one of the bar stools at the breakfast bar, and Grace took that as a sign he was listening. 'I came across this programme, where you can volunteer,' she said. 'They're looking for people with skills in certain areas.'

'That's me out, then. I don't have any skills.'

Grace gave Seb the 'look'. 'Actually you'd be perfect. They're looking for people who can help out with a form of art therapy.'

'Ah,' Seb said, not seeming that interested.

'They have various schemes all over the world, some working with disadvantaged kids, and some working with kids who are refugees.'

'All over the world?' Seb echoed, and Grace knew she had him interested now.

'Yep. Some in this country, and some as far away as Africa and the Middle East. But you could stay here if you wanted to.' Her eyes sparkled; she knew that staying in London was the last thing Seb wanted to do. He had never really travelled; had never really been well enough to.

'Africa would be cool,' he said, trying to hide his excitement but not succeeding very well.

'I brought some of the leaflets with me. They're in my bag if you want to have a look.' Grace watched as Seb made a great show of finishing his juice before slipping off the stool and casually strolling over to her bag, which she had dropped on the sofa on her way in that morning. She returned her attention to the lunch, and then hands reached for her waist and she was pulled away from her kitchen duties.

'You're supposed to be asleep,' she said to Adam with a laugh.

'The smell woke me.'

She wriggled from his arms so she could look him in the eye.

'The delicious smell, obviously,' he added with a cheeky grin.

'You need to sleep. You've worked crazy hours this week.'

'I'm a doctor. I'm supposed to work crazy hours.' Grace watched as he poured himself a glass of fresh juice. 'And besides, I'm intrigued — you said you had something to tell me.'

'That can wait,' Grace said as she turned to start peeling carrots.

'And you are avoiding the subject.'

'Maybe, but I think I'm probably not the only one with something to tell you.' She indicated Seb, who was sitting on the sofa, completely oblivious to the fact that Adam was up and about. He was entirely engrossed in the information that Grace had brought him.

'You can't distract me, Miss Taylor. I have ways of making you speak.'

Grace laughed as Adam reached for her again and began to tickle her. 'Stop!' she said breathlessly. 'I'll tell you, but right now I need to focus on making lunch. Go speak to your brother.' Adam raised his eyebrows in question, but Grace didn't want to steal Seb's thunder. 'Go on — Seb will tell you all about it.'

Adam leaned in for one more sneaky kiss, then plonked himself down beside his brother. 'So what's up, bro?'

Grace couldn't help but congratulate herself on her idea. She had not seen Seb this animated in an age.

'Don't you think it would be awesome?' Seb said after he had told Adam about the opportunity, practically wriggling in his chair like a small excited child.

'Sounds great, Seb, really. But what about college?'

'Well, I finish in May. I can defer uni for a year, no probs.'

Adam nodded, clearly taking it all in.

'I've got it all figured out,' Seb said. 'I can go and experience life — you know, real life. And help people, help kids. I gotta do something, Adam. Life's just not working for me right now. I think Grace might be right — I need to do something completely different. Focus on helping other people; get out of my own head.'

Adam looked at Grace, and for a moment she could not interpret his expression. She wondered if he were cross with her.

'Grace is usually right,' he said, and broke in to a smile. 'And I haven't seen you this excited since I took you to see the last *Star Wars* movie.'

Seb reached over and punched Adam on the arm, who then made a great show of being mortally wounded. 'So if I arrange a meeting, will you come with me?' Seb asked, all serious again.

'Of course, mate. You have my schedule. Any time I'm free, I can be there.'

'I need a guardian to sign off on my application, since I'm not eighteen yet.'

Grace froze. She knew it had all been going too well. Seb assumed that as Adam was his older brother, he could sign as a guardian. What he didn't know was that since Seb had living parents, only they could sign an official document. Adam was not his legal guardian, and the likelihood of their father signing off on a trip — let alone one to Africa

— was almost nil. She could have kicked herself. If she had just waited another eight months! She risked a glance at Adam and could see that he had figured out the glaring problem, too. With the slightest shake of his head, he sent the message to Grace that they could talk about it later. Right now they were going to let Seb enjoy the moment.

8

Grace and Adam had left Seb at home while they went for a walk in the local park. 'I'm so sorry, Adam,' Grace said as soon as she was sure they were out of earshot.

'Don't be. It's a great idea, but I doubt my father will go for it.'

'I should have thought it through,' Grace said, wringing her hands a little. 'Seb can't go to Africa, not with his medical problems. I'm such an idiot!'

'You're not an idiot, Grace, honestly. You're right, it's just what he needs. He's so wrapped up in his own head sometimes, and he can't see the transplant as a gift. All he can see is that someone died and now he is alive.' He ran a hand through his hair, making it stand up at funny angles — another thing that Grace loved about him. 'I just need to figure out how to persuade

Father.' He sighed. 'Worst-case scenario, Seb will have to wait for eight months. Once he's eighteen he can pretty much do what he likes.'

Grace watched as a frown crossed Adam's face. 'What?' she asked.

'Just wondering if Father will pull the same trick on Seb as he did me.'

Grace waited, wondering what on earth Adam's father had done in addition to everything else.

'You know — withhold money, if you don't do things his way. He was never very happy about Seb studying art. He might threaten not to pay for uni if Seb insists on volunteering abroad.'

'He would really do that?' Grace asked, even though deep down she knew that Adam's father had all the power in the family.

'He's never been like that with Seb before. I mean, with me, yeah; but not him. But then Seb was so sick for so long, I think Father would have let him get away with anything.'

'But that's not true anymore,' Grace

finished Adam's thought aloud.

'Seb will always have medical issues, and needs to be careful. But he's not fragile now, not like he was. I want him to have a life, you know?'

Grace nodded and reached for his hand.

'Otherwise, he's right. What was the point of his transplant? He should be able to live his life how he chooses. When he was a kid he was so restricted, but that's not true anymore.'

'Well whatever happens, we'll support him. We can help him with uni. It'll be tight, but we can do it.'

'What did I do to deserve you?' Adam asked, and pulled Grace into his arms.

'I was just thinking the same,' Grace whispered into his chest. They stood there together, neither wanting to break the magic of that moment.

'As lovely as this is, I believe you have something to tell me,' Adam said. With one final kiss he stepped away from her. 'Enough of my family drama. Let's talk about you'.

'I'm not sure if now is the right time,' Grace said, suddenly nervous. Today had been a bit of a trial already, and she wasn't sure she was ready to add to that.

'Enough prevaricating, Miss Taylor. Tell me now, or I won't treat you to a hot chocolate,' Adam said, indicating a coffee barrow who seemed to sell hot chocolate with all the trimmings.

Grace took her time pretending to decide between the two, but was really just trying to give herself a few more seconds to work out how to explain it. Finally, she sighed and said, 'Okay, well . . . Monsieur Bonevere has offered me first violin.' She held her breath as she waited for Adam to reply, then found herself being spun around and looking into Adam's surprised and smiling face.

'Gracie, that's fantastic! A dream come true! Why wouldn't you want to tell me?'

'Because it's with the San Francisco Chamber Orchestra.' She quickly found that her feet were back on the ground.

'And that would be . . . ' Adam said, his smile having faltered a little.

In America,' Grace finished Adam's sentence, and waited for him to process the news.

9

Grace watched as Adam took a step away from her, and tried to read his expression.

'First violin in a world-famous orchestra, Grace. It's everything you ever wanted.'

Grace bit her lip and nodded. Despite her fear of telling Adam, and what that might mean for their future together, she couldn't help but be excited.

'That's fantastic, Grace. Really wonderful.'

'You might want to tell your face that.' She smiled, but this time it was tinged with sadness. Perhaps she had been worrying about the past for nothing — perhaps this amazing opportunity was going to be the thing that broke them up.

'Sorry,' Adam said, rubbing his hand across his face and then managing a smile. 'It was just a bit of a surprise.

Well, not really a surprise. I mean, I heard you play the other night, and you're amazing . . . '

Grace felt his gaze find her.

'I'm waffling. Sorry.' He took hold of both of her hands. 'I knew you could do it. From the first day I met you, I knew you'd be one of the greats of this world.'

Grace shook her head to try and fight down the slight embarrassment she felt at his words. 'It's a great opportunity, Adam, really it is. And I'm honoured, but I haven't accepted it yet. I wanted to talk to you, to see what you thought.'

'You're not serious.' He dropped her hands and ran a hand through his hair. 'Grace, you can't turn them down! This is your dream.'

'I didn't say I was going to. I just have a lot to think about.'

'Like what?'

'Well, us for a start.' She watched as Adam turned away from her and wondered what that meant. Did he just see their relationship as a bit of fun — nothing serious; something they could both walk away from should something better, be it person or opportunity, arise?

'No, I won't let you,' Adam said.

Grace could feel her eyebrow rise and she knew that she was giving him the 'look'. She took a breath before answering, not wanting to answer in anger. 'Well it's not really up to you.'

'Grace, this is an amazing chance for you. It's what you always wanted.' He looked upset, and Grace wasn't sure whether it was because she might be leaving or because she had misinterpreted the strength of his feelings.

'So you don't mind if I go live on the other side of the world.' She thought she would be able to keep her voice level, but it cracked as she said the last few words. She focused her eyes on her feet, not wanting to see Adam's face or try to read his thoughts. A hand found her chin and he gently but determinedly forced her to look upwards.

'Grace, of course I care, but I won't be the reason you don't get to have what you want.'

'I'm not sure you get a choice in that,' Grace said, her small smile mirroring Adam's.

'I thought I cost you your dreams before. I won't again.' Grace watched as the smile faded and was replaced by knitted eyebrows.

'What do you mean?' She thought she could guess but wanted to be sure.

'All I could think of after you left was that I had ruined your life. If I'd left you alone, you would have stayed at Henry Tyndale and been able to follow your music.'

'But I did follow my music.' Adam had turned away from her now, so she reached out for his hand and made him face her.

'You didn't go to the Royal Academy, though.' Grace's face reflected the question mark in her mind. Adam shrugged, seeing her expression. 'I checked their class list each year, looking for your name.'

Now Grace was surprised — not by Adam blaming himself for her leaving school, but because he had kept tabs on her musical ambition. 'I found another way,' she said. 'The Academy was part of my dream, but really it was about being able to play in an orchestra. It might have taken me a bit longer, but you might have noticed I just kind of made it.' She smiled again and hoped he would join her.

'No thanks to me,' he said, and there was no smile.

Grace sighed. They really were going to have that conversation. 'It wasn't your fault, Adam David Needham. Are you listening to me? It was not your fault.' She said the words slowly and carefully.

'You said that already.'

'I'm going to keep saying it till you believe it.'

'Well, you are very annoying.' And now they both laughed.

'You said it yourself — we were kids. If you want to blame someone, blame the system, the teachers, the board, or Arabella. I don't know; maybe global warming fried everyone's brains.'

'Has anyone ever told you that you're crazy?' Adam said.

'You have, a few times.' She squeezed his hand. 'It's the past, Adam. It's done. We can't change it.'

'Yep, you're right.' Grace allowed herself to be pulled into Adam's arms. 'So, Miss Taylor, how do you feel about long-distance relationships?'

'They're okay. I mean, absence makes the heart and all that, but I have an alternative proposition.'

'Are you breaking up with me?'

Grace giggled at Adam's impression of an angst-ridden teenage girl and then elbowed him in the ribs. 'No! I just wondered how you feel about the American healthcare system.'

10

Grace could barely contain the urge to skip along the road. She and Adam had spent all night making plans and drinking hot chocolate at their favourite all-night coffee shop. Adam had needed some time to get his head around the idea of working abroad; but as Grace pointed out, there were plenty of opportunities in America, and his current post would be coming to an end in the next few months. Grace felt like she needed to pinch herself just to believe that it was all real; that all of her dreams were coming true. She was meeting Pria and Katie for a late breakfast and she couldn't wait to tell them. She knew they would thoroughly approve!

She pushed open the door of the café and was immediately aware that her friends were waving frantically at her from a corner table.

'Over here! Quick! Quick!' Katie said, practically jumping up and down in her chair. Grace took her seat and the waitress magically appeared.

'She'll have a full English and filter coffee,' Pria said before Grace could open her mouth or even look at a menu. 'Well we all know what you need after being up all night,' Pria said impatiently and at the same time waving the waitress away imperiously.

'Pria!' Grace said, a little embarrassed at the behaviour that reminded her so much of her time at Henry Tyndale.

'I'm sorry . . . I just have to know how it went.'

'I don't think I even need to ask — I can tell by your face!' Katie squealed.

'Let her speak,' Pria said sternly, but her eyes sparkled.

Grace shrugged, trying to appear nonchalant. 'It went fine,' she said vaguely, but she could not contain her grin any longer. 'It was perfect! I mean, he was surprised, but so genuinely pleased for me.'

'Of course he was. He is the perfect man,' Katie said dreamily. 'A man who thinks your dreams are as important as his.'

Pria rolled her eyes and then gave Katie the benefit of a particularly sharp elbow. 'Let the girl speak. Enough fairy tales!'

'But it *is* a fairy tale!' Katie said, and Grace had to nod her head in agreement.

'He wants to come with me; we're going to go together.' Grace thought her heart would burst. The only word that encompassed how she felt was joy. 'I can't believe it's all working out so perfectly.'

'Well you deserve it, honey, you really do,' Pria said just as three very large English breakfast plates arrived. 'To Grace and her happy-ever-after!' The three of them clinked their coffee cups together in a toast.

★　★　★

The three days that Adam was away seemed to drag, but Grace forced herself to keep busy; there was, after all, a lot to do. She had been researching everything she could about San Francisco — the best areas to live in, places to visit and eat, and most importantly what hospitals were in the area and what programmes they had for doctors. She couldn't wait to show Adam all that she had found out. She wanted to surprise him, but she also couldn't wait to have someone to share her excitement with.

She was making her way to Adam's flat when her phone beeped. She knew without looking that it was a text from Adam.

'Change of plan.' It said. 'Meet me in the park?'

'OK,' Grace sent back before retracing her steps.

When she got to the local park, she could see that Adam was already there, which was strange since she would have been nearer than he was if he'd come from home. She walked quickly, no longer eager to tell him all her news. Now she was concerned.

'Adam!' she shouted. It was not something she would normally do, and a group of teenage girls turned from their phones to stare at her for a moment.

Adam turned, and she had a lurching feeling in her stomach that something was wrong. She had only ever seen Adam like this two times before, and both of them were when Seb was gravely ill. As her mind raced, she broke in to a run.

'What is it?' she asked breathlessly when she was within a few paces of him. 'Is it Seb?' she asked again, since he had not answered her first question.

'No, Grace, Seb's fine. He's at the flat.' Adam patted the seat beside him and she sat down. All her joy seemed to have evaporated. If it wasn't Seb, then it had to be something equally as bad.

'Adam, please tell me. I'm really starting to worry here.'

'It's not bad news, really, Grace. Just a bit of a change of plan.' He smiled, but Grace knew that it was forced. It wasn't reflected in his eyes, which were crinkled with worry.

'*Our* plans?' Grace asked quietly. She could barely bring herself to say the words.

'I've had some time to think about it, and I think we may have got a bit carried away.'

'I think the apartment overlooking the Golden Gate Bridge is probably a bit of a stretch, even with both of our incomes,' Grace said, hoping to make him laugh; desperate for his words not to mean what she knew they did. But he didn't laugh, and Grace's heart sank. 'You aren't coming, are you?' Someone needed to say the words, and Adam didn't appear able to. She turned to look away. How had she got it so wrong? Adam had seemed so enthusiastic. She was sure she hadn't misread that, yet after only three days he had completely changed his mind. The thought struck her like a slap. Three days that he had spent with his father. Of course; now it all made sense.

'Your father doesn't want you to go.'

'It wasn't his decision, Grace.'

She shook her head in disbelief. 'Last week we were making plans and were so excited. Are you saying I imagined that? You said it was just the change and the adventure you were looking for.' She didn't bring up the end of the conversation, where he had told her that he could not believe he was going to get to share it with her, the woman he loved. She could not say those words aloud.

'No, of course not.' He reached out for her hand, but seeing her face, seemed to think better of it. 'I just had some time to think, and rationally it's not the right choice for me now, career-wise.'

'But I looked into the programmes at the local hospitals, Adam. There would be great opportunities for you out there — just like there are here, but probably even better.' Grace knew she was being foolish. The decision had been made, and she was unlikely to persuade Adam to change his mind and go against his father's wishes. 'But none of that matters,' she added, unable to keep a hint of bitterness from her tone, 'because once your father's made up his mind, that's it.'

'That's not fair, Grace,' Adam said, looking stricken.

She hated to see him like that, and knew the one she was really angry with was his controlling father. 'Maybe not, but it just seems strange to me that you were all for our arrangement until you spent some time with him, and now all of a sudden you've done a one-eighty.'

Her mind was in turmoil. There was so much more she wanted to say, but she didn't know where to start. She didn't want to give up without a fight, but she had the feeling that she had already lost the battle.

'What about Seb?' she said. 'I'm sure your father had a few things to say about his plans.' She forced herself to look at Adam, and she didn't need him to answer; she could see it all over his face. At least he had the grace to look slightly ashamed.

'He isn't going either.' Grace shook her head as she listened to him speak. 'We should never have suggested it. He has too many medical issues to go off to the developing world. It just wouldn't be safe.'

Grace's mind flooded with all Adam had said in the past about Seb needing to live his life, to get out there and just do it. How could so much have changed?

'But he's going to take part in a project in this country,' Adam went on. 'Probably in London, so he can carry on living with me and still go to university.'

'I take it he still gets to study art, like he wants to.'

'Of course. My father is overprotective of Seb, I know that, but he loves him and he wants what's best for him.'

'And what about you, Adam? What

does he want for you?'

'He wants me to be a great doctor; to follow in his footsteps.' Now he did take her hand. 'It's what I want, too, Gracie.'

'I thought you wanted me.'

'It doesn't change anything, Grace — or at least, it doesn't have to. If anyone can make a long-distance relationship work, it's us.'

Grace wanted to believe him, but she knew the truth. It would be difficult and they would drift apart, their lives moving in completely opposite directions, in different time zones. 'Have you told your father about us?' she asked.

'He's known for a while. He was the one who suggested we slow down a bit. I mean, what's the rush? If we want it badly enough, and if it's meant to be, then we'll make it work.'

'I'm going to be on the other side of the world.'

'We can text, email, and skype.'

Grace stood up. She needed time to think and she couldn't do that here, with Adam.

'Grace, my father is right. We can make this work.'

She turned to him, her anger flaring, as well as the desire to tell him what his father had done all those years ago to keep them apart. Adam stood, too.

'Face it, Adam, your father would do anything to keep us apart.' The anger curled inside her and she wanted to let it go, to tell him everything. But she knew that she wouldn't, however angry she was. Seb was right: if Adam knew, it would drive a permanent wedge between him and his father; and Grace could not live with the knowledge that she had torn them apart.

'That's not fair, Grace. He just has a pragmatic take on life.'

'Only where I'm concerned, it seems. What is it that he doesn't like about me? That I was a scholarship girl? That my parents both had to work to pay the mortgage? Or does he think music isn't a worthwhile profession?'

'He doesn't have a problem with any of those things.' Adam's voice was cold now, and he took a step away from her as if he wanted to physically distance himself from her comments. 'He just wants to make sure that you're serious, before I go throwing my career away.'

'He thinks I'm not serious about you? How could he possibly know that? He's never even met me!' Her voice was raised now, and people were starting to take notice, but she didn't care.

'You've got him all wrong, Grace. He was right the last time; he just wants to protect me.'

'What do you mean, he was right the last time?'

'When you left school, my father made a deal with me. He said that if you cared, really cared, then you'd write to me, try and keep in touch. He said that if you did, I could write back and we could keep seeing each other. But if you didn't, I'd know you weren't serious about me and that I should move on.'

Grace stood frozen to the spot. All the anger was melting into shock. To make a deal with his son, to seem so fair and reasonable, but then to manipulate the situation to his own aims . . . Adam's father was beyond controlling. He was cruel.

'I'm not telling you this to make you feel guilty, Grace. That's the last thing I want. We were kids, and you had a lot to deal with at the time. We're adults now, and our relationship is totally different. But perhaps my father's right. If we spend some time apart, we'll know for sure how we feel about each other.'

That was the final blow — to hear those words, those doubts come from Adam's mouth, and not been able to tell him the truth . . . It was too much.

'I have to go,' Grace mumbled. Then she fled, hearing Adam calling her name as she ran.

11

Grace's phone beeped. She fought the urge to throw it across the room. It would be another message from Adam. He wanted to talk; he wanted to see her. She knew he was right, but she couldn't be in the same room with him. If she were, she knew she'd tell him. It would cause a rift with his father that could never be repaired, not to mention what it would do to Seb, and Grace could not live with that responsibility. The guilt would eat her up, and her relationship with Adam would be soured by it forever.

But it wasn't Adam this time. It was a message from Seb, asking her to meet him for coffee. 'Maybe another time,' she wrote. 'I'm busy practising a new piece.' She hoped that would be enough for him to get the message.

Another beep. 'It must be a very quiet one.'

Grace frowned. How could he possibly know that? Then she rolled her eyes. With a sigh, she hauled herself off the sofa and moved towards the front door of her flat. She caught sight of herself in the mirror and nearly jumped in fright. Her hair was a complete mess and, worse than that, was in desperate need of a wash. She was wearing her oldest and most comfortable tracksuit bottoms and T-shirt, and had managed to drop last night's ice-cream all down her front without realising. She had to admit to herself that she was a bit pathetic.

She unlocked the door and pulled it open, hoping she'd get Seb inside before any of her neighbours spotted her dishevelled state.

'I knew it!' Seb shook his head in mock disappointment. 'What is it with girls when they have an argument with their boyfriend? It's like the ultimate excuse to eat junk.' He wrinkled his nose. 'And jeez, when did you last take a bath?'

Grace grabbed him by the front of his jacket and pulled him into her flat. 'It was a bit more than an argument. Coffee?' she offered, moving towards the kitchen. She watched as Seb surveyed the kitchen, which was in desperate need of some attention. Well, he and Adam weren't exactly housekeeping stars themselves.

'Why don't we go out?' Seb suggested. 'We can grab some food, and we're less likely to catch something in a place with better hygiene standards.'

Grace punched him lightly on the arm. 'Fine, we'll go out. But I'm buying.' She reached for her bag, but Seb gently lifted it off her.

'Err, not until you shower and change. I have a reputation to maintain, and I can't be seen with someone in such a state.'

'Aren't you the little comedian today.'

'Someone has to be. I'm living with Mr Grumpy at home.'

Grace swallowed. She hated the idea of Adam being unhappy more than she did her herself. She had to force down another wave of helplessness. What could she do?

'I'm literally wasting away here,' Seb said, his voice cutting through her thoughts.

'Easy, Tiger! Give me five.' Grace headed towards the bathroom.

'Probably should make it ten,' Seb said, not even bothering to look up from his phone.

Grace grabbed a pillow from the sofa and tossed it as his head, which he managed to duck without even pausing in his texting.

★ ★ ★

Forty minutes later, Grace was watching Seb devour a huge cheeseburger. 'Not that it's not nice to see you consume food at a quite frankly alarming rate,' she said, 'but what's going on, Seb?' She watched as he swallowed his latest mouthful.

'Adam's miserable, and from what

I've seen you're miserable too, or maybe becoming one of those hoarders. You know — they never go out, and they never clean; they just kind of hoard stuff.' Grace just looked at him. 'Okay, maybe not a hoarder. But you really might want to tidy up a bit, or other people might start thinking that.' He glanced up from his meal but quickly looked back down, and Grace knew he was avoiding whatever it was that he wanted to say.

'You know this is complicated, Seb. I'm not sure what I can do about it.'

He took a napkin and wiped his mouth. Grace watched as a battle raged across his face, and she felt such overwhelming concern that she reached across the table for his hand. 'It's not your fault, Seb.'

He looked at her. 'Yeah, it kind of is . . . again. It seems I have a real talent for making the people I care about miserable.'

'Seb — ' Grace said, but he held up his free hand to stop her.

'You need to tell him, Grace. The truth. All of it.'

She shook her head. 'No way. I can't, Seb; you know I can't.'

'Why? So my father can have an easy life? So he doesn't have to face up to choices he's made and keeps on making? Choices have consequences, Grace.'

She leaned back in her chair but held on to Seb's hand. She had never seen him so angry or confused. 'Seb, what's happening?' She said it softly. There was so much pain going around, and now it seemed that Seb had been pulled into it. She wasn't sure she could bear it.

'It's Adam,' he said, and Grace felt her heart lurch.

'I know he's upset right now, Seb, but he'll move on. We both will. We've done it before.'

Now it was Seb's turn to give Grace the 'look', quite possibly for the first time ever. He didn't need to say the words. Grace knew that she for one had never completely got over losing Adam the first time, and she was guessing that Adam was the same.

'It's more than that,' Seb said.

Grace waited, but he had fallen silent and was now shredding his paper napkin. 'Seb?'

'He's changed,' Seb almost blurted it out. 'He always stood up to our father, even when it cost him. I never had to do that. Father would pretty much do anything to keep me happy and healthy, and I could usually talk him round to whatever it was I wanted.'

Grace nodded. Now she thought she understood, and felt a pang of guilt. This bit of upset was definitely due to her. 'Adam told me your father said no to the volunteering abroad. I'm really sorry, Seb. I should never have suggested it.'

'Yes you should!' Seb raised his voice, and for a moment the staff of the coffee shop stopped what they were doing and stared in their direction. Grace gave them a reassuring smile to indicate that all was well.

'I'm glad you suggested it. But it's not about me, Gracie, it's about Adam.'

'But he said he thought your father was right — that going abroad, especially somewhere like Africa, wasn't a good idea.'

'That's just it. Don't you see?' Seb slouched back in his chair, clearly exasperated, but Grace still wasn't sure why. When she didn't answer his question, he leaned forward and continued. 'He's never backed down before. I don't mean he's always won. My father usually gets what he thinks is right, but what he never gets is Adam agreeing with him.'

Grace nodded. She thought she was starting to understand.

'He's given up, Gracie. It's like he's so tired of fighting Father about everything that he just decided to start going along with him.'

Grace sighed. It was certainly not like Adam, but she couldn't blame him. Her own parents had always been so supportive of her. Of course they had expressed their opinions over the years, but she had never had to fight with them about the things that really mattered to her, like her music.

'What are we going to do?' Seb asked her.

'I'm not sure what we *can* do. Have you talked to Adam?'

'That's the worst part. I've always been able to talk to him, always, about anything; but it's like he's actually turned into my father. He doesn't listen to me, and — '

'What?'

'He actually told me I was too young to understand!'

Grace put a hand over her mouth to hide the smile that she was fighting back.

'Are you laughing?' Seb said, sounding scandalised.

Grace moved her hand and tried to compose her expression without much success. 'I'm sorry, Seb, really. I just can't believe he said that!'

'I know.' Seb's face relaxed, and then

he was grinning too.

'Its way worse than we thought,' Grace said, and now Seb laughed. She relaxed a little, glad that she had managed to break the tension. But it didn't change the facts. 'So do you have a plan?' she asked, feeling like she might need to brace herself for whatever Seb was about to say.

'He wants to see you.'

'I know, but I still don't think we should tell him about the letters. You know it might cause a rift between him and your dad. You need to think about that.'

'I've thought about nothing else, Gracie. I feel like I'm losing Adam, the *real* Adam, and I can't; I just can't.'

'And you think the truth would be better coming from me?' Grace said, wondering if Seb wanted her to play the 'bad' guy by telling Adam news that was sure to cause him pain.

'No!' Seb said, looking shocked. 'I think we should do it together. I mean, I think *I* should tell him, but I was hoping that you could be there. I know Adam will want to see you.'

Grace took all this in. She could feel emotions rage inside of her. There was fear, and anger at Adam's father, but trepidation about telling Adam. Adam might never speak to his father again after he'd heard the truth; and she wondered if, when his anger had faded, he would blame her for tearing his family apart. However, Grace decided that none of this took priority over Adam losing himself, and she knew what she had to do.

12

'Seb, you're going to wear a hole in my carpet.' Grace handed him a cup of coffee and indicated that he should sit down. He took the mug but continued to pace. 'It's not too late to change your mind, you know,' Grace told him, and her words had the desired effect. He stopped pacing, and his look told her he was going to go through with it. She smiled and tilted her head in the direction of the sofa, and with some effort he sat down. When the doorbell rang he jumped up like he had been caught out doing something he shouldn't, and in the process slopped coffee all over the rug.

'Sorry!' he said, leaving his mug on the table and running for the door.

'Don't worry, I'll sort it out.' Grace's voice sounded long-suffering, but in truth she was glad of a few extra seconds to compose herself before she had to see Adam again. It had been nearly a month since that day in the park, when her perfect dream had started to crumble.

'Seb! What are you doing here?' Grace could hear Adam from her spot in the lounge, as she used a cloth to soak up the spilt coffee.

'Is Grace here? She said she wanted to see me.'

'She does. We both do.'

* * *

Adam stepped into the lounge, and the sight of him nearly took Grace's breath away. He was casually dressed in chinos and a striped shirt, his hair was fashionably messy, and only his slight frown marred the image. 'Hi,' she said, at a loss for words.

'Hi,' Adam echoed, his voice uncertain now. 'Are the two of you planning something?'

'No,' Seb and Grace said together

with perfect timing.

Adam raised an eyebrow. 'Sure looks like it to me.'

'We do need to speak to you about something,' Grace told him. 'Do you want anything to drink or eat?'

Adam shook his head and then sat down. Grace perched on the arm of the sofa, and Seb took up a seat across from him. 'Okay, now I feel like I'm in trouble,' Adam said.

'We're worried about you,' Seb blurted out.

'Okay, any particularly reason?' Adam enquired in a calm manner that Grace felt sure he used with overly anxious patients.

'You're turning into Father!' Seb seemed as surprised by his own comment as Adam did.

'Because I agree with him for once? Look, buddy, I know you're upset about the volunteering thing, but we aren't saying you shouldn't do it. In fact, Father agreed it was a good idea — you just need to be closer to home, where there's medical treatment if you need it.'

'It's not about that,' Seb said.

Grace looked between the two of them and wondered if the conversation was going to end in a fight. Seb was definitely right — Grace had never heard Adam talk like this, and certainly never where Seb was concerned.

'Then what *is* it about?' Adam asked.

Seb looked at Grace, and the helpless look on his face indicated that he wasn't sure what to say next.

'We're both worried about you.' Grace said.

'I miss you, Grace, and I hate not seeing you,' Adam said. Then he turned to Seb. 'I'm sorry if I've been hard to live with, but I'm sure Grace and I can talk things through and find a way forward.'

'Not until you know what happened!' Seb jumped to his feet and turned to Adam. 'He's been lying to you — lying for all these years, and you just don't see it.'

Adam held out his hands to placate Seb. 'Wait — what are you talking about?'

'Grace wrote to you.' Grace had to look away; she didn't think she could bear to see what that simple statement would do to Adam.

'What do you mean?' Adam's tone was flat and lifeless, and Seb took a step back, unsure of whether he should keep going.

'When I left Henry Tyndale,' Grace said, 'I wrote to you. Every day, for a long time.'

Adam stared at her, and she could feel the confusion and pain pouring out of him. He shook his head. 'You never wrote to me.' He sounded so young and hurt that Grace wanted to pull him into her arms, but she knew she needed to finish the story.

'Every day,' she repeated carefully. She could feel the tears fighting to be released, but with effort she held them back. 'For months. And I never heard anything back from you. Eventually I made myself accept that I'd never see you again, so ... I stopped.' That wasn't the whole truth, but Grace could not bear to add to his pain. In actuality, she had continued to write, telling him about her life and how much she missed him. She no longer posted the letters, however, but kept them in a box under her bed.

'But I never got them,' Adam said. He looked from Grace to his brother. 'Seb?' But Seb wouldn't, or couldn't, look at him. Adam grabbed his arm. 'Seb?' he said again.

'He kept them from you.' Seb's voice was shaking, and Grace could only watch helplessly as tears rolled down his cheeks.

'Father,' Adam said.

'I'm so sorry,' Seb said, his voice muffled as Adam pulled him into his arms as Grace had seen him do many times at school.

'It's not your fault, bud. Not your fault.'

'I should have told you before.'

'You told me now.'

Grace felt as if she were intruding on a private moment. She turned away.

'Grace,' Adam said quietly.

'I'll leave you two in peace for a while.' With that, she disappeared into the bedroom.

Before long, there was a knock on the door. 'Gracie? Can I come in?'

She stood with her head leaning against the door. She wanted to be with Adam, and talk to him, but she could not shake off her fear of the consequences.

'Grace, please.'

She swallowed and pulled open the door.

'Seb hasn't stopped apologising, but I should be the one making apologies. I should never have believed you wouldn't have tried to keep in touch.'

'I'm sorry, too.'

He shook his head. 'This is Father's fault, not yours.'

'Please don't say that, Adam. That's why we didn't tell you. I don't want this to tear you apart from your family.'

'You can't seriously expect me to just ignore this! Are you saying I shouldn't be angry?' There was distance between them, and it was not just physical.

'No, of course not.' Grace tried to stay calm. She knew that Adam was angry and had a right to be. 'I just think you need to take some time to think about this before you speak with him and say something you'll regret.'

'You know what I'm the most tired of, Grace?'

She shook her head, knowing that nothing she could say at this moment would be right in Adam's eyes.

'I'm tired of being told what to do.' His eyes flashed.

'I understand that.' She reached out a hand for Adam's arm, but he shook it off roughly.

'You *don't* understand, Grace. All these years I thought he'd been so reasonable! I actually thought he had my best interests at heart. But he lied.'

'I know he kept my letters from you, but I'm sure he believed he was doing

249

the right thing — that he was protecting you.'

'None of it was about me! It was all about him.' The fight seemed to have gone out of him and he flopped down onto the bed, head in his hands. 'He made a deal with me, Gracie. He said he was worried that I felt more for you than you did for me. He said that if you wrote to me or tried to contact me, then we'd both know you really cared.' He looked up, and Grace could see the pain in his eyes. 'He said if you wrote to me, then I could write back. We could see each other; be together.'

Grace felt like her heart had stopped. She shook her head as she tried to make sense of what she had just been told. 'I don't understand.'

'He said I could see Seb if I agreed to his deal. I was so sure you'd write to me, and he knew that, so I agreed. I actually said yes. But he knew he'd get what he wanted, because he already had it all planned out. Don't you see? From the start, he knew I'd never get your letters — because he was taking them!'

The truth hit Grace, and she felt like she would shatter into a thousand pieces. All the time they had lost when they could have been together . . . all the pain that could have so easily been avoided.

'For all I know, my mother was in on this!'

Grace managed to find her voice. 'Adam, no — I'm sure she'd never agree to such a thing.'

'You don't know my father.' And with a grimace, he stormed away down the hall. When Grace finally composed herself, she walked out to the lounge to find that both Adam and Seb were gone.

13

Grace pulled her front door to and locked it for the last time. There had been a lot of 'lasts' in the past few weeks. She had said goodbye to Pria and Katie, been home for one last weekend with her parents, and packed all her furniture up so that it could go into storage. Now all she had to do was drop off the keys with her landlord and wait for her taxi to the airport. She had said all her goodbyes but one, and she was sure now that she wouldn't get the opportunity. She had sent Adam more texts than she could count, and heard nothing. She had tried ringing his mobile, but only ever got his voice mail. Seb answered her texts but gave only minimal information. All Grace knew was that Adam had confronted his father and that things were not good between them.

She sighed as the all-too-familiar

feelings of guilt welled up inside her. As she had suspected, the truth had caused a rift between Adam and his father and indirectly separated her and Adam as well, as surely as the secret had threatened to do. Grace had tried to tell herself that it was a no-win situation, and that perhaps she and Adam were just not meant to be; but her heart was having none of it. She had loved Adam as a teenager, and she knew she still loved him; but she also knew it was something she would have to learn to live with, again. It wasn't like she hadn't had years of practice.

A horn sounded, and the cab she had booked pulled up at the kerb. The driver got out and lifted her suitcase into the boot. Grace opened the back door and got in. The driver eased the car into the rush hour flow — and then braked so suddenly that if Grace had not been wearing a seatbelt, she would have landed on the floor of the car.

'What the — ? Is he trying to get himself killed?' the driver exclaimed.

'Hello, Gracie,' Adam said as he climbed in beside her.

'Mate, get out! I'm booked.' The taxi driver's voice brought Grace back to the present.

'Err, its fine,' Grace said. 'He's with me.' She turned to face Adam, who somehow managed to look both sheepish and quite pleased with himself. 'Always with the drama,' she said, unwilling to voice any of the thousand other thoughts in her head.

'At least I didn't need to save Seb this time.' Adam's smile was contagious.

'How is Seb?' Grace asked, thinking it was a safe topic, but all the while aware that they had only the forty-minute drive to talk before she left for the other side of the world.

'He's good. He's Seb,' Adam said with a shrug.

Grace could stand it no longer. 'What are you doing here, Adam?' When he didn't answer, she continued, 'I'm on my way to the airport. You know, leaving for the States.'

'I know that. That's why I'm here.'

'You haven't answered a single text or phone call, Adam, and now you leap into my taxi when I'm leaving the country.' She turned now to look at him to see if she could read his thoughts on his face.

'Yeah, sorry about that. Lots been going on.' Grace waited for him to elaborate, but he didn't.

'That's all you have to say?' Grace was starting to feel angry. Her heart had leapt at the sight of him, she had to admit, but now she was feeling like he was playing some kind of trick on her.

'I love you, Grace.'

'OK. I love you, too, Adam. But I'm not sure now is really the time to start getting into this . . . ' Adam held up his hand and Grace stopped talking.

'This is exactly the time.' He reached out for her hand and she let him take it, despite her sudden desire to protect herself from more hurt that the memory of his touch was sure to bring. 'I love you. I always have. My father has done everything he could to keep us apart, but I'm an adult now and I make my own choices.' He lifted her hand to his lips and kissed it. 'I'm yours, if you still want me.'

'But I'm leaving. I know you think that a long-distance relationship could work, but in my opinion we'd just be saving up the pain for later.'

'Well I was thinking we could share an apartment, but even if I was down the block I'm sure we could cope.'

Grace stared. She was sure she had fallen asleep and was dreaming.

Adam's face broke into the broadest of grins. 'That is, if you still want me to come with you?' His smile faltered just a little, and Grace knew he was sincere. 'Well?'

'Of course!' Grace squealed. 'Of course I want you to come. But what about a job, and all your stuff, and — ' Grace was silenced with a kiss that left her breathless.

'Seb is meeting me at the airport; he has my bags. And I have a job, Grace.

That's what I've been doing these last few weeks.'

'Why didn't you tell me any of this?' She was trying to decide whether to shake him for putting her through the pain of the last few weeks or to kiss him again.

'I didn't want to disappoint you; I wasn't sure I could get everything sorted. My father seemed to be under the impression that if he could stop me getting a job out there, I'd stay. But he was wrong.'

Grace felt a coldness fill her. She knew she couldn't let Adam throw away his career. 'You can't give up on medicine, Adam. You can't, and I won't let you.'

'I'm not. I couldn't get a job with any of the major teaching hospitals, but Father's influence doesn't stretch as far as the less prestigious institutions.'

Grace shook her head. He couldn't do this. They would find a way; they would make a long-distance relationship work.

'Gracie, look at me. It's fine. I got a job at a hospital that looks after people with little or no insurance. They have a free clinic and everything. Don't you see? It's what I've always wanted to do — to help people who really need it. My father was set on me being a surgeon like him, and I thought it was what I wanted too, but it isn't. I *know* what I want — and quite possibly for the first time in my life, I'm going to have it.'

Grace let herself be kissed again, and for a moment she couldn't focus on any of the questions she wanted to ask. 'I never wanted to get between you and your Father, Adam,' she finally managed to say after pulling away.

'You haven't. I've told him what I want from life and what I'm going to do. It's up to him now. He needs to decide what's more important — his dreams for me, or my own.' He undid his seatbelt, then pulled her into his arms and kissed her hair. 'Don't worry — Seb is sure he'll come round, and he's usually right. Also, he's promised to work on him, and Seb is certainly persistent.'

Grace giggled. She let out her breath, feeling like she had been holding it in for an age. 'Is this really happening?' she whispered.

'I don't know, Gracie. Do dreams really come true?'

She wiggled in his arms so she could see his face clearly. 'I guess they do . . . I guess they do.' And then she kissed him, confident in the bright future ahead.

We do hope that you have enjoyed reading this large print book.

Did you know that all of our titles are available for purchase?

We publish a wide range of high quality large print books including:
**Romances, Mysteries, Classics
General Fiction
Non Fiction and Westerns**

Special interest titles available in large print are:
**The Little Oxford Dictionary
Music Book, Song Book
Hymn Book, Service Book**

Also available from us courtesy of Oxford University Press:
**Young Readers' Dictionary
(large print edition)
Young Readers' Thesaurus
(large print edition)**

For further information or a free brochure, please contact us at:
**Ulverscroft Large Print Books Ltd.,
The Green, Bradgate Road, Anstey,
Leicester, LE7 7FU, England.
Tel:** (00 44) **0116 236 4325
Fax:** (00 44) **0116 234 0205**

Other titles in the
Linford Romance Library:

INTRIGUE IN ROME

Phyllis Mallett

Gail Bennett's working holiday in Rome takes an unexpectedly sinister turn as soon as she arrives at her hotel. Why does the receptionist give out her personal details to someone on the phone? Who is the mysterious man she spies checking her car over? Soon she meets Paul, a handsome Englishman keen to romance her — but he is not what he seems. And how does Donato — Italian, charming — fit into the picture? Gail knows that one of them can save her, while the other could be the death of her . . .

THE FAMILY AT CLOCKMAKERS COTTAGE

June Davies

Feeling bereft after her sister Fanny gets married and moves away, young Amy Macfarlene must manage Clockmakers Cottage on her own, while earning a living as a parlour maid and seamstress for a wealthy local family, the Paslews. Her wayward brother Rory is a constant concern, as he is clearly embroiled in some shady dealings and refuses all offers of help. Amy's childhood sweetheart Dan is a comfort to her — but as her friendship with the handsome Gilbert Paslew grows, so do her uncertainties about her future . . .

RACHEL'S FLOWERS

Christina Green

Rachel Swann takes a sabbatical from her London floristry job to come home and temporarily manage the family plant nursery. But then it emerges that her uncle has also asked the globetrotting plant collector Benjamin Hunter to do the self-same task! Wary of Ben's exotic plans for the establishment, Rachel is determined to keep the nursery running in its traditional manner. But as the two work together, they cannot ignore the seeds of a special relationship slowly blooming between them . . .

UNEASY ALLIANCE

Wendy Kremer

Joanne is intelligent, capable — and beautiful. Her female colleagues always assume this plays a major part in her rapid promotions, no matter where she works, and now all she has to show for her efforts is her current state of unemployment and a string of short-lived jobs on her CV. Signing up with an exclusive dating agency, she meets tycoon Benedict North — an exceptional, charismatic man. But when she finally lands a job, Joanne is unsure of whether there is room in her life for him — despite her growing feelings . . .

WEDDING BELLS

Dawn Bridge

Marina is attending her widowed father's wedding when she is immediately drawn to handsome fellow guest Roberto. A romance soon sparks between them, but it's anything but smooth sailing ahead when Marina discovers her old flame, Jon, has lost his memory, and visits him in hospital. Torn between trying to help him and spending time with her new love, Marina is distraught. Can she and Roberto overcome their difficulties and find happiness together?

CHRISTMAS IN MELTDOWN

Jill Barry

When her assistant suddenly quits, struggling bistro owner Lucy is filled with despair. Top chef James rides to the rescue — but Lucy fears he's hijacking her menus. As electricity fizzes between the two, and festive delights fly from the kitchen, Lucy faces a business dilemma. Does James hold the key to success? Snow poses fresh challenges as each cook falls more deeply in love with the other. Will it be James or Lucy who melts first?